Shattered Yesterdays

SARAH LOUISE DALE

SARAH LOUISE DALE

The Sweet Tea Mama Publishing
Shattered Yesterdays

Sarah Louise Dale
(RENAMED) Shattered Yesterdays Published by
The Sweet Tea Mama Publishing (2023)
Original Cover Photo by Sandralise via DepositPhotos
Final Photo Edit by Sarah Louise Dale via Canva Pro using Cormorant
Garamond Bol Fonts.

ISBN: 978-1-7320114-4-1 (eBook)
ISBN:978-1-7320114-5-8 (Paperback)

To the ONE person who fought me on this rewrite more than anyone else.

Chapter One

Time stood like a breath of air before it fanned out into the atmosphere. Parker sat in the wooden high-back chair fit for a king, where the weight of the crown on his mop of brown hair caused his head to hurt. He scanned the crowd, hoping to see her watching as he listened to the Duke of Norfolk spout some nonsense about his niece. Parker Warrick only had eyes for Gabby Lawson.

Gabby was the Anne Boleyn to his Henry the VIII, in the early days when passion ran rampant in their relationship. He loved her more than he ever thought possible to love a woman, but he wasn't sure how Gabby would take the news he was about to drop on her the moment the play ended. This was night two of *Shakespeare's Henry VIII*, and after last night's performance, his life changed.

The sun set behind the backdrop of the platform and stars dotted the darkening sky. He smiled when it came time to deliver his next line, his character wretched with anguish. Gabby wasn't in the play; she was the host of the evening. When Parker ended his scene, he left the stage as the lights blackened to set up for the last scene. He rushed to her; as his boots swished through the damp grass from last night's rain.

"Hey beautiful," he said, sneaking a quick kiss across her pale cheek. He brushed her long brown hair over her shoulder. She pushed him away, laughing.

"Parker, you've got to get back out there."

"Okay, fine. But once the Princess Elizabeth is baptized, you and I need to find a quiet place to talk. I've got big news!"

"I can't wait," she said, before he took his place on stage.

The lush grounds of the Nano Springs Inn made the perfect spot for the town's community play. Gabby managed the small bed-and-breakfast, and they hoped to buy it from the current owners in a few years. Well, Gabby wanted to own the Inn. Parker preferred a much more active lifestyle than the Vermont small town offered. Something else they'd need to talk about, but all in due time.

While they both grew up in Nano Springs, Gabby enjoyed the picturesque main street shops and countless people waving, even if they don't know you. But they do know you because well, that's small-town living. Parker needed lights and action. He wanted to feel the noise vibrate through his bones and meet different people every day. Parker didn't pretend he wanted what she did, but with this new opportunity, he had to see what else was out there.

The standing ovation and applause echoed against the trees and shook him to his core. He craved it like a drug, and it was like he'd spent the past five years in withdrawals. Parker reluctantly said goodbye to everyone and turned to meet Gabby inside the six-bedroom inn.

Because they weren't married, Parker kept an apartment downtown. Sometimes they got away with spending the night together, but he knew his mother valued her reputation in town, so he tried to respect her when it came to possible scandal.

Though these days who wasn't shacking up? When his father died of a heart attack his senior year of high school, it was up to him as the oldest son to take care of his mother. He took that role seriously, and it was Scarlett Warrick who'd encouraged him try out for the community play.

Gabby blacked out the week of the summer play for down-time at the Inn which left them alone once the attendees went home. Parker pulled his bag from his car, letting it hit his leg with every step, and carried it up the wooden stairs. At the door to the room on the third floor, he paused as the bathroom door slowly opened. Gabby sashayed across the room, and he stopped to admire the way her white gown brushed against her toned legs.

Parker thought about marriage from time to time, even thought about enlisting his brother Jacob and Gabby's best friend Christina into the plans. If he was honest, commitment scared him. Jacob mentioned a while back it was only a piece of paper, but Parker knew Gabby didn't see it that way. She was too traditional, minus the sleeping together part.

What if he failed her? What if he failed himself? Mistakes are easy to make, but hard to fix. There was still time. At least that's the lie he told himself every day. Most women wouldn't wait as long as Gabby waited, and she focused on her career, for now.

Parker didn't feel pressured into anything with her. She accepted things and moved on about her day. Situations like a disgruntled guest who didn't like his room, or the washing machine releasing too much water, would send him over the edge, but not Gabby. She'd smile and assure the guest had what he needed, kick the washing machine, and move on.

A volcano of nausea fluttered in the pit of his stomach as he watched her climb into bed. She smiled that smile that melted all his resolve and patted the mattress beside her.

"Wanna join me, Your Majesty?" she asked, her head cocked to one side.

Parker tossed his bag in the corner and stripped down to nothing. Gabby pulled the chain on the lamp, covering them in complete darkness. Minus the tiny sliver of moonlight peeking between the curtains, he couldn't see a thing. He slid in beside her and she lay her head on his chest.

"I love you, Parker," she whispered.

He bent down and brushed his lips across hers. The nausea went away, and desire stirred deep within. They needed to talk, but they had the night, and he wouldn't let anything come between them.

As they lay breathless after, he thought about calling the agent who approached him the night before and cancel everything. The idea that there was something exciting waiting for him in L.A. stopped him from changing his mind.

Ripples from the rock she'd tossed across the lake, moved like lines on a tear-stained notebook page. This was their spot; they talked about everything here, the good and the bad. This was one of the bad. She couldn't believe he was leaving, as if five years together were nothing more than an opportunity. Like she was nothing more than a placeholder. Parker swore it was only for six months, but she knew and heard the underlying truth hidden behind his words. Six months would turn into a year and so on and so forth until their relationship crumbled like the rough draft of a novel.

Gabby tried to understand his desire to go to L.A. and give the career a shot. Parker played a convincing Henry VIII, but a T.V. show? It wasn't even the same thing. A classic Shakespeare play vs a small screen pilot that may or may not even take off? It was as if he didn't think things through before saying yes.

4

They'd spent so many hours right there on the dock overlooking the massive lake, talking about settling down and how nice it would be once the inn was theirs. Now this?

"Will you please say something?" he asked, leaning against the railing of the dock. She watched from the corner of her eye as he picked splinters from the wood and flicked them into the water.

Gabby opened her mouth but released a cough instead of all the things she wanted to say. She swallowed and tried again. "Parker, I'm trying to understand where all this is coming from. Why not tell me the other night when Marcus approached you?"

From the corner of her eyes, she saw his head hang loose over his hands. "Gabby, I'm sorry. I should have said something sooner, but if I did, would your feelings have changed?"

She scoffed. "Yes. I would have had more time to convince you to stay here with me." In her head, the line reeked of immaturity. She was surprised she didn't stomp her foot and pout.

Parker shifted to wrap his arms around her. The breeze ruffled her hair as a trout jumped in the water nearby.

"Answer me this," she said, "did you ever want to be all in with me?" Gabby needed to hear him say it. He needed to own the truth of how he really felt about the lifestyle she thought they'd both wanted.

"Come with me," he said, whispering in her ear. "We could try something new before settling down here in Nano Springs." He couldn't even give her a straight answer. She didn't want to go with him to a smog-infested state that held so many people who didn't think about anyone but themselves.

Gabby shoved away from him and started walking off the dock toward the side of the house where she parked her car. She couldn't believe he would even suggest her leaving the Inn. For the last four years, Gabby put every ounce of energy into making the place successful, as successful as a small business could be, anyway. The owners would soon move to a retirement home closer to their children in Florida. The couple's children agreed to honor their wishes and transfer ownership over to Gabby when the time came. That time was so close she could taste it. Purchasing a whole business wasn't easy though, especially once Parker stopped kicking in his share. She should have seen the signs then.

"Gabby, wait!" Parker jogged beside her and placed a hand on her arm. She wanted to shrug it off but turned to face him. His sharp jawline drew him to her like a moth to a candlelight and it was all she could do not forget their fight and beg to be kissed. No. She had to hold her ground.

"Wait for what, Parker? If you're leaving in the morning, you should probably pack your bags. I'm going to visit my parents for a little while. I don't want to talk about this anymore with you." Gabby didn't wait for him to say anything else as she rushed to the car and slammed the door. The air conditioner blasted from the vents, hitting her face like a breath of fresh air, only colder.

The drive to her parents' house wasn't a long one, but she enjoyed the winding road to her parent's cabin on the other side of town. The trees on either side swayed in the wind and, as a distraction, she pushed the button to lower the windows. Nano Springs sat at the heart of Vermont and was such a peaceful place to live. The small town of five hundred made for close-knit relationships and comfort. Main street passed by in a slow blur, reminding her of why she stayed in her hometown after graduation. The slow pace was everything she wanted and asking for more than that would be sinful. Even before Parker, she imagined raising a small family of her own there.

As she pulled into her parent's driveway ten minutes later, she killed the engine and took a moment to gather her thoughts.

Claire and Andy Lawson were the perfect example of marriage done the right way. While she was an only child, they raised her to appreciate life and be kind to everyone. It was only fitting she went into the hospitality industry. L.A. was not the place for a six bedroom inn, and Parker was crazy if she thought they could make that work.

Gabby got out of the car and slammed the door shut with more force than she intended. Cursing under her breath, she twisted a hair tie she always wore around her wrist. The elastic band was especially helpful with the anxiety filled moments. The sting brought her back to the present. Gabby stepped onto the porch of the small two-room cabin and knocked before entering. What greeted her on the other side of the door made her blush.

"Oh! Sorry," she said, hiding her eyes behind her hands. "I can come back later."

"Nonsense. It's good to see you, dear," her mother said, fluffing her hair. She swatted Gabby's father away before greeting Gabby in a soft hug.

"Everything okay, hon?" her father asked. He stepped around his wife and wrapped his arms around her. Andy sensed her moods far better than any father she knew, and she welcomed it, especially on a day like today.

"Parker's leaving." Gabby sat on the sofa in the quaint living room and explained everything. How an agent spotted him at the play two nights ago, invited him out to audition for the pilot of a T.V. show, and what she felt was a false promise of returning home in six months' time.

"Parker loves you, honey. You need to give him more credit than you are right now," her mother offered. Claire wore silk slacks and a matching blouse, her traditional work clothes having just come from the youth intake center in town. She slipped off her flats and joined Gabby on the couch.

"He wanted me to go with him," she said, swiping at a tear on her cheek. Since he broke the news to her that morning, she hadn't shed a single tear and now it's like a faucet turned on and everything came out. "What if he gets out there and decides he likes it and never comes back? I can't leave Nano Springs; my life is here. You are here," she cried. Gabby gave up on keeping her face from getting wet and just let the tears fall.

Andy squatted down in front of her, his knees strong as a young man, and placed his hand on her leg. "Sweetheart, you can't live life wondering about the what ifs. Doing so will hold you back from promises of the future and you don't want to live like that, do ya?"

"I know, Dad," she said, placing her hand on his. "I'm just scared."

Andy stood and pulled her into his arms. "It's okay to be scared, but it's not okay to let that hold you back. Give him a chance. The guy might surprise you. He may get out there, realize he can't live without you, and come rushing home to you. You'll never know if you don't give grace and support."

Gabby knew her parents meant well and said as much. They left her to go start lunch in the kitchen and she thought about what it would mean for Parker not being around as much. It hurt, because they'd hadn't spent more than a day or two apart since they started dating. But he was going to go with or without her approval.

After having lunch together, she thanked her parents for listening and called Parker from her cell on the way back to Nano Springs Inn. When the call went to voice mail, she tossed it in the seat beside her. They had tonight and with a single text welcoming him to the house that evening; she shook off the doubt and let it blow in the wind through the opened windows of the car. What could happen in six months?

. . .

Parker swiped his cheek one last time with the blade before wiping the excess shaving cream from his jawline. He gazed in the long bathroom mirror and as he explored his brown eyes; for the thousandth time he wondered if he was making a big mistake. Gabby didn't take the news as well as he'd hoped and now, she was off at her parents, probably telling them what a horrible boyfriend she's got. Of course, Gabby's parents would talk her down, but would he still have a girlfriend?

When the agent cornered him behind the curtains on opening night, he thought the guy was joking. The man, dressed in an expensive suit you couldn't buy in Nano Springs, gave off this positive vibe as he shook Parker's hand. Once he told him about the show, Parker couldn't help but steal some of the man's eagerness to get him to L.A. Parker would shoot a pilot for a new spin-off show. Apparently, Hollywood was still in this era of taking old shows, gender swapping them, and making new shows.

Gabby wasn't wrong, though. Small town community play versus the pilot of a T.V. show was like living in two different worlds. Looking back in the mirror, Parker used a nearby wash-cloth on his face and left the bathroom. Laying open on the small bed in his apartment over the pharmacy was a small suit-case. The agent assured him they'd take care of any needs he had once he was in California.

As a child, Parker didn't have a real aspiration of what he wanted to be when he grew up. His mindset was that the right career would come to him when the timing fit. Little good that did him now, at twenty-six years old. Gabby seemed content having him help around the Inn with repairs. The tasks were simple, and he thought it was the right job for him. Now, he wasn't so sure.

Once he zipped his bag, he sunk onto the mattress, causing a creak to echo against the near empty room. He needed little when he spent so much time with Gabby. A photograph of the two sat on the nightstand. Parker picked it up and stroked a finger across Gabby's face. They were on the dock last fourth of July, fireworks exploded in the background.

He loved her, but the pull to see where this new adventure would take him was so strong. It was a chance he had to take, and Gabby could either accept it or they'd move on. A sharp pain shot across his chest at the idea of them breaking up. Parker took a deep breath and placed the photograph back on the nightstand.

His phone pinged with a message. A smile spread across his face as he read the three short lines. Grabbing his suitcase and zipping it closed, he flipped off the light and made his way down to the car. If he could convince Gabby they'd be together again in six months, then he could drive away from Nano Springs with no guilt. In her message, she'd given him the chance. Now all he had to do was take it.

Gabby stirred the lemonade in the pitcher and gazed out the kitchen window. The room was small, but it didn't need to be big when she was the only one who cooked. The guests enjoyed the patio for breakfast, or the dining room for dinner. Tonight wasn't about the guests though, tonight was about saying goodbye to the man she loved.

On her way home from her parents', she decided she would let herself cry and get all the sadness out, but then when it came time for him to leave, she'd smile and support him. It was the hardest act she had to play, and she wasn't even the actor.

Once she tossed her purse onto the check-in table just inside the door; she began texting everyone, Jacob and Scarlett Warrick and Christina. Gabby could never do this without her best friend. Luckily enough, Christina was dating Jacob so it was easy to get them both to the inn. They all text back words of comfort and promised they'd be there soon.

The sun was setting over the lake when she carried the lemonade out to the patio. Parker walked up the stairs as she let the screen door bang shut behind her. When he smiled and motioned with his hands an offer to help, Gabby gently shook her head and looked away. She couldn't let him see how weak he made her feel. She wasn't crying because she wasn't angry anymore, no the pain she felt went much deeper than that.

"Thank you all for coming by. As you all know by now, Parker is leaving us in the morning. Since his flight is so early and he'll need to leave before dawn, I thought it would be nice to all get together before he left us."

She tried to keep her voice calm and understanding, but she struggled against all the emotions sitting like a sore on her heart. Tonight would be hell. How do you pretend to be happy for someone when you aren't? Gabby wasn't the fake-it-til-you-make-it kind of woman. She focused her eyes on Christina and took a deep breath. Thank God for best friends.

When she told Christina the news, her friend did what she always did and tried to get her to see the other side of things while still being supportive of her feelings. The problem wasn't that she didn't know the other side; it was that she didn't want to see it. She and Parker were meant to be together. Six months was a long time, especially considering where he was going.

"Snap out of it," Christina whispered in her ear. They shared a bench at the table. Christina was right. Spacing out wouldn't change anything. For the rest of the evening Gabby focused her attention on Jacob and Parker and let their conversation carry her away. Jacob reminded Parker not to get an ego while he was off becoming famous. You could hear the pride for his brother in the younger Warrick's voice, but at least he wasn't being immature as he was known to be. His antics were popular among the familiar crowd.

Scarlett promised she'd send him home- baked goods, the kind that only came from her kitchen. As a children's author, Parker's mother was usually off on book tours and conferences. When she wasn't selling books away from Nano Springs, she could be found in her kitchen baking for the whole town.

The crickets came out to sing their song and the sun disappeared behind the horizon. When the second batch of lemonade was gone, Gabby thanked everyone for coming and watched them all walk to their cars to leave. Parker started to speak. Instead of letting him say anything, she turned and kissed him. She was done talking, for now. Morning would come quick, and she didn't want to waste the night going back and forth about something she couldn't control.

As she lay breathless in the moon's glow later that night, a white sheet wrapped around her naked body, she made a vow to herself. Gabby would give Parker the six months; but that meant phone calls every night before bed, and video chats at least once a week. It was a compromise she could handle, barely.When he asked what would happen if the show took off, she shrugged and told him they'd cross that bridge when they needed too. For now, he'd have her support. There wasn't much else left to say after that.

Chapter Two

Parker stepped off the plane at LAX, nursing a pounding headache. Eight hours with a toddler kicking his seat wasn't his idea of fun. Now in L.A, he'd let himself soak in the California sunshine he'd heard so much about. Once they could deplane, he grabbed his carry-on and exited into the aisle as fast as he could. The roar of a nearby engine caused the breezeway to stink of exhaust.

Marcus told him he'd be getting off the plane at Terminal one and meeting him at Parking Level one. There, an agent would wait with a car to pick him up. He didn't need to go to baggage claim since he only had the carry-on, so he eagerly walked through the crowded airport. Parker couldn't wait to leave.

He passed a Vera Bradley store, a News Stand, and a coffee shop before crossing the connector bridge from the terminal to the parking garage. At the exit of the bridge stood a tall, lean woman with the most gorgeous hazel eyes. Everything was perfect about her; he couldn't see not one flaw. She smiled a movie star smile and waved a sign with his name on it. Her red hair was in a long, slick ponytail at the base of her neck. She wore a black pantsuit that fit her curves in ways he'd never seen before.

"Parker?" the woman asked. Her voice was cheerful and welcoming. She greeted him with a light kiss on the cheek before slipping the cardboard sign under her arm. "It's so nice to meet the person Marcus couldn't stop raving about. "Let's get out of this stuffy garage."

"I was expecting Marcus. But thank you for meeting me here. I'm out of my element." Parker tried not to look like a loser with no confidence. He failed. The term star-struck is something he'd only heard of, but not until now, did he understood the meaning of the term.

"Well, I'm Sasha House. I'm an executive for the network and volunteered to bring you in to the studio. I hope you don't mind going straight there?" Sasha crossed the parking lot, making a beeline for a black BMW series 3. The car alone made the trip worth it. Anyone driving a car like that in Nano Springs would be driven right out of town. Too rich for their blood.

Sasha seemed to have a flavor for the color. "The director wants to meet you and he's already been on set longer than he wanted. Sadly, it's how things work out here. We go when we're called."

"Not a problem at all." Parker wiped sweat from his brow before tossing his bag in the back seat. He slipped into the passenger seat and buckled up. Sasha reeved the engine and exited the parking garage onto a busy street. Parker would have to get used to how active everything was in L.A. Wasn't that the point, though? The excuse he gave Gabby before he left. He needed an active lifestyle. Now he had it, but it's what he wanted. Right?

"Are you excited about being here? Marcus said you're coming from a blip on the map." Sasha zipped through traffic. She looked over at him, gripping the door frame, when the car came to a stop at a traffic light. "Oh, sorry," she said, laughing. "We drive fast here too."

Parker drew in a deep breath and caught her scent. Lavender mixed with something that smelled like clean linen. Hell, he didn't know. She just smelled nice. He had to remind himself the woman sitting next to him wasn't his purpose for being in California. Forgetfulness could destroy his life faster than Sasha's crazy driving.

"If I'm being honest," he said, loosening his grip on the door. "I'm nervous. I came out here to prove something, and I intend to stick it out until the end." He didn't leave behind the love of his life for nothing.

"Yourself or someone else?" Sasha asked, stopping at another light. Traffic lined the streets at a near standstill. In Vermont, they called it five o'clock traffic. Except, it wasn't five, and it was California.

"Left a girl back home. Long story." He didn't want to divulge his relationship problems to this gorgeous stranger. But when she asked him about Gabby, he couldn't help but lay out everything that bothered him about her not joining him. By the time they arrive at the studio, Sasha knew everything. Their first meeting, his marriage fears, and Gabby's dreams for the little inn back home.

Sasha was quiet as she gathered her purse from the backseat. When Parker unbuckled his seatbelt, she placed her hand on his arm. Something stirred in him when she gave his arm a gentle squeeze. Desire? Need? He wasn't sure. Since Gabby, it had been ages since someone made him feel those things.

"Parker, it's okay to have a dream of your own. To go after something you want. To live a life you enjoy. Never hold yourself back. Your future looks bright right now."

He thought about what she said as they left the car. Sasha made some good points. Gabby was his world, but was it healthy to put that on her shoulders? She had the business and her family and friends. He shouldn't feel guilty for seeing where this acting gig went.

A huge number six was painted in black on the front of the building. Sasha opened the door and ushered him inside. The set was unlike anything he'd ever seen. It put the stage play scenes and platforms to shame. A warehouse was separated into sets; a home, school, and even a hospital. The plot of the show was a remake of an older show. While the original main character was a female, but he'd be taking over the gender swap role. He'd die and come back in someone else's body. He couldn't wait to see how the show turned out.

"Ready?" Sasha asked, looping her arm in his. "Let's go live your dream, Mr. Warrick."

Gabby peered over the steering wheel of her rented Honda and watched as Parker paused on the sidewalk in front of a white stretched limo. He threw his head back and laughed, his smooth tone reaching her where she sat two cars behind. When he leaned over and caressed the cheek of a petite blonde woman, Gabby almost lost it in a sea of tears. She had to admit; the woman was attractive.

A limo driver stepped forward to open their door and waited for the couple. Gabby couldn't hold the tears inside any longer when she watched Parker lean in and captured the woman's lips with his own. His hands rested on the woman's ass, and he pulled her toward him.

Gabby gasped and swiped her brown hair from her face. Embarrassed beyond belief when she realized she was not in L.A. but in Vermont at her desk. She had a few hours to herself now that last night's guests had checked out. The dreams were becoming more frequent each day that passed. Another day with no phone call. Gabby knew Parker landed and made it to the studio.

She'd seen the photo outside the studio door he'd posted on social media. The post was a vague notice to everyone on his friends list that he'd arrived. She begged Jacob and Christina not to say anything online.

A month later, and he still hadn't called. Other than the one post, Parker hadn't been active online either. His phone went to voicemail the first week and then disconnected since then. Gabby pounded a fist on the wooden oak desk. Parker didn't want to live in Nano Springs. There was no point in trying to force that idea anymore.

The screen door creaked open in the foyer, startling Gabby from her seat.

"Hey, lady." Christina poked her head around the doorframe, waving a cup of coffee.

The room had no door after they converted it from a sitting room to a check-in area. The paneled walls made the place seem dated, but Gabby loved the authentic charm. A big bay window overlooked the expansive front yard and circular driveway.

Gabby glanced outside and saw Christina's SUV parked next to her car. Good, she was alone. Gabby didn't know if she could handle seeing the new lovebirds together. Gabby loved that Christina found someone that looked at her the way Parker used to look at her, but the two were publicly R-rated these days.

"Hey. Have a seat. About to make a bank run, but I got a minute." The chair opposite her side of the table was plush and comfortable. A typical check in day was quick and easy. Still, Gabby wanted to add comfort to the place, too. Over time, she added more of her own touches to the inn, and this one made the vibe of her home comfortable.

"Still nothing, huh?" Christina's face fell when she plopped into the seat. "Gabs, you look like you haven't slept in years." Christina never minced words.

"Nope."

"Let me take you out," Christina said, tapping the desk with her knuckles. "You and me, Joe's Pub, and a few vodka sours. That should do the trick."

"Christina, alcohol isn't going to fix this," Gabby said, shoving the week's receipts into the bank envelope. "My boyfriend ghosted me, and I've had no closure. I'd much rather have a pint of ice cream and sob into my pillow."

"Well, hello Ms. Hallmark Movie. Come on, Jacob is on call with the fire department tonight and it's been a while since we've gone out. You don't have to drink."

Gabby found nothing on the calendar to prevent her from going. She sighed and agreed to meet Christina at Joe's after dinner. The new guests would check in shortly. The Inn offered a small dinner option as part of their stay. Once she was done with that, her night was completely open.

"Dress nicely, 'kay? We don't need to tell the town you're mourning Parker. He doesn't deserve to have this effect on you, so don't give him the win." Christina stood and met her in front of the desk. When she wrapped her arms around her neck, Gabby choked back a sob. Having to navigate this new normal wasn't easy. Two weeks wouldn't be a big deal if the dead air wasn't so clear. Four weeks and counting was pushing her limit. It wasn't until the day before that she realized how dependent she'd become having Parker in her life. Was she always that needy?

A few hours later, with errands complete and the guests settled, Gabby prepared for a night out. The navy blue dress fit the curves of her body and hung in a flair at her calves. She braided her hair into a bun and dabbed a subtle layer of make-up on before driving to the town's only bar. Time for neediness ended tonight.

The end of summer meant the gravel parking lot of Joe's Pub had more cars than usual. Locals were returning from visiting the beaches along the coast and tourist were going home. At least until Winter when the locals and tourist would come together to enjoy the snowy mountain activities. The sun faded and as small as Joe's appeared on the outside, the action inside was a totally different story.

Landon Marshall sat on a barstool, sipping a luke-warm beer. His blonde hair draped over his dark eyebrows, covered the wrinkles that formed there over the last two weeks. He was neither a tourist nor a local, and if he were being honest with himself, he didn't quite know what he was anymore. Lost? Maybe. The little town he stumbled into a few days ago offered charm and distance. Distance from the pain, hurt, and guilt.

The music blared from the speaker at Joe's, drowning out the surrounding conversations. Other than a few shop owners and the Airbnb host, he'd avoided human interaction as much as possible. The bartender slid another cold beer his way. With a nod of his head, Landon twirled around in his seat to scan the bar.

Near the front door, next to a poorly position dartboard, stood two attractive ladies his age. The blonde escorted the reluctant brunette over to an empty table. Landon couldn't hold back a smile as he realized she was just as miserable. He didn't revel in her misery, but it was nice to know he wasn't alone.

The blonde sauntered over in his direction. Did she notice him watching? Was she going to make a scene? He was going to offer an apology, but he didn't need to. She bypassed him and stepped up to the bar a few feet away.

"Hey, Jamie. I didn't know you'd be working tonight."

The bartender wore a dark leather jacket and had that rugged look about him. One that would scare someone from the city. And he did. His gruff voice didn't lessen those fears.

"Hey, Christina. Good to see you, hon. Dragged our sweet girl away from the inn, huh? Any word?" Jamie asked, setting up glasses to make a few cocktails as if they were regulars.

Landon couldn't help but lean in a little closer, though making sure he wasn't obvious.

"Nope. The bastard hasn't updated social media, sent a text, or made a phone call at all. Jacob is mad as hell, too. Ready to hunt his brother down and beat him senseless," she said, laying down a credit card. "Gabby will be alright though. We'll take care of her. Going to show her a good time tonight." Christina leaned over the bar and swiped a washcloth from the sink on the other side. "I'll be right back for our drinks."

Landon pulled from his beer. The things you hear at a small-town bar. Break-ups, protective friends, and good times. Can't heal a broken heart in a bar, though. If so, Landon wouldn't be contemplating his third beer. He motioned for the check and drained the bottle.

"Third night in a row. If you don't watch yourself, people will start thinking you're from here," Jamie said, handing him a receipt. He smiled and leaned against the bar on his forearms. "Care to open up a bit?"

"I don't know what you mean." Landon placed a credit card on the thin strip of paper.

"What's your story?"

His story? Landon didn't think the old bartender would want to hear about his reasons for being in town. Even for bar talk, his past wasn't something he wanted to divulge in tonight. Besides, who wanted to hear about how the love of his life took her own, utterly shattering his happiness?

Nah. He'd pass on the free therapy.

"Needed a change of scenery," Landon said, signing the receipt. He dropped the pen with a thud. "Nice place you got here." He needed to divert the man's attention from himself. Jamie launched into the history of Joe's Pub. Landon couldn't focus. He was drawn to the brunette. Landon tuned out after Jamie mentioned his grandfather built the place with his bare hands.

He turned his attention to the women at the table in the corner. The way her face fell as she looked hopeful at the door every time it opened, as if she were waiting for someone who would never come. Despite her friend's upbeat personality, and the drink sitting before her, the brunette refused to perk up. He didn't know her story, but he knew how it felt being somewhere you didn't want to be.

Jessica took everything from him. The future they'd planned together, the home they'd bought after college, even the car that sat in the driveway. But that wasn't the worst thing she stole.

He didn't realize she was beside him until the sleeve of her blue dress brushed against his arm. Her closeness startled him out of the memories he couldn't seem to avoid, no matter how far away he ran. The fabric sent chills down his spine, and he realized he wasn't quite ready to leave the bar.

"Hey there. Can I buy you a drink?"

Chapter Three

G abby started at the sound of his voice, and she didn't miss the glare Jamie gave the man who had spoken. When she turned to decline his offer, she paused. Something in his sea-green eyes told her not accepting would be a mistake. His golden hair needed a good brushing, but it was his eyes that had her wanting to know everything about him.

What was she doing? Gabby felt the warmth crawl across her skin as she realized she was staring. God, she was being ridiculous. Before she could say anything, Christina rushed to the bar and stole her attention.

"Gabby, I gotta run. Mom is having some sort of breakdown and is tearing apart her kitchen." Christina rolled her eyes. It wasn't uncommon for Mrs. Riley to have episodes, nor was it new that her daughter had to come calm her down. "Jamie," Christina said, smiling at the man behind the bar. "Care to close us out?"

Gabby peered at the man who offered to buy her a drink. "I'll catch up with you later. I think I'm going to hang around a bit." She threw her arms around Christina's neck and said, "Thanks for getting me out. I needed this."

Christina eyed the man wearily. "Okay. Make good choices." Gabby blushed at the look she gave her before turning to leave.

Once her friend left the bar, Gabby turned her attention to the man and held out her hand. "I'm Gabby. It's nice to meet you."

"Landon. Nice to meet you too," he said, taking her hand.

The softness of his hand sent electricity into the air, or so it seemed.

"So, drink?"

"Here ya go, Miss Gabby." Jamie slid a fresh vodka sour across the bar. "I'll be here if you need anything."

Gabby rolled her eyes. "Thanks Jamie." She took the drink and a napkin. "Let's find a table away from prying eyes." She led him to an empty spot at the back of the bar. The crowd was growing and the noise with it. She didn't think they'd be able to talk much, but it was flattering to have a man buy her a drink.

Parker was gone. She needed to accept he wouldn't be coming home soon, or at all. The silence he gave her was deafening. A month isn't a long time, but he promised to call every day, a promise broken for a month now. A man buying her a drink wouldn't hurt. It's not like she was cheating. A drink was a drink, right?

Besides, Jamie was at the bar with his eyes glued to the back of Landon's head. Jamie cared for her like his own daughter, and he wouldn't let things get out of hand.

Gabby placed her drink on the table. Once seated, she let herself look into his eyes again. He wasn't from here, that she knew. She'd spent nearly all her life in this small town and could spot a newcomer faster than anyone. From the suntan and blonde hair, she imagined he was from California or Florida. Somewhere with a beach and lots of sun. The wrinkles at the corners of his eyes told her he'd stumbled on hard times in his life.

"Thanks for humoring me with a drink," he said, sipping his own. She noticed he didn't get a new beer, which was both intriguing and slightly suspicious. God, she needed to get over herself. He wasn't out to take advantage of her. She was so far off her game, a game she hadn't played in years. It was like she forgot how to talk to the opposite sex. *What is wrong with me?*

"To be honest, I didn't want to come here tonight. But now I'm not quite ready to go home." Gabby took a sip of her drink and gazed around the bar. A lot of the locals waved and smiled her way. They probably talked behind her back, but not in the cruel way most gossips do. They knew Parker as much as they knew her. His absence wasn't lost on them either.

More and more people entered the bar, and it was almost getting too loud to hear, let alone talk. They spent some time sharing stories of where they grew up and their day. Gabby loved hearing about how nice her neighbors were to strangers who came into Nano Springs. A lot of places outside of Nano Springs were popular for shunning newcomers, and Gabby liked not being embarrassed by her town.

After a while, the volume got to be too much. She took one long gulp of her drink and placed her hand on his arm. "Wanna go for a walk?" A grin spread across his face, and she froze. "I mean, an actual walk. Not like code for anything dirty." *Oh God, shut up, shut up now.* She covered her mouth with her hand.

Landon laughed and finished his beer. "It's okay. How about the trail in the park at the center of town? It's my favorite spot here so far."

They paid the tab and said their goodbyes. Jamie gave her a look of apprehension, but she mouthed an "I'm okay" before following Landon out the door. Having people care about her gave comfort where sadness lingered. Even without Parker, she'd be okay. As time passed, she saw it more clearly.

A mile long park sat in the center of town and held a few gazebos and little ponds with bridges. Gabby visited this very spot every day for a mental health break. The paved trail that circled the park gave her the exercise and mental clarity she needed. Lately, she'd come by more than once a day.

The moonlight reflected off the rushing water beneath the small wooden bridge. They stopped on the bridge, and both silently leaned against the railing. Gabby searched her brain for how to pick up the conversation again. With Parker, things were never this hard, but he was more social than Landon seemed to be.

One day he'd walked into the inn where she was working during the last Summer before college. He said, "hi," she said, "hi", and that was about it. Nothing magical or romantic about it. As she watched the lightning bugs dance atop the water now, she tried to remember what drew her to him. His charm, for sure. Parker was good at saying the right things. It wasn't until now that she realized maybe they weren't as compatible as she thought.

Of course, these troubled thoughts could be the alcohol mixing in her system.

Landon cleared his throat and nudged her shoulder. Gabby tucked a strand of her hair behind her ear. She still didn't know what to say, no matter how many times she opened her mouth to speak.

Thankfully, Landon must have noticed her discomfort, because he angled his body to face her. "I'll tell you my story if you tell me yours." While he offered a small smile, he stared at her so intently that she stumbled over her words. The man was a flirt, but not arrogant, as if he knew he could get whatever he wanted. The notion that her feelings mattered after living for a month questioning so many things overwhelmed her.

"I didn't mean to upset you." Landon took a step back, his hands up in front of him.

"No. It's not you," Gabby assured him, tugging his arm towards her. "Let's just say it's been a really long time since someone took my feelings into consideration." Landon relaxed beside her, and she could tell he was waiting for her to go on. And she did. Gabby told him about Parker's opportunity. She admitted that when Parker went to L.A. it caused her to reevaluate everything about their relationship.

Embarrassed, she laughed a gentle laugh and shook her head. The hair she tucked behind her ear earlier fell and settled against the side of her face. "Well, I guess one thing you've learned about me tonight is that alcohol is like truth serum. Now you know all my secrets."

Landon reached over and brushed her hair away from her face. The gesture was soft, kind, and felt sincere. "I doubt I've learned all your secrets, but thank you for sharing with me."

Gabby took a deep breath and shook out the tension that had tightened on her shoulders.

"You're beautiful. I'll tell you that right now," Landon said, straightening against the railing. "So tell me now, because I'm not a fighter unless I need to be. Will Parker be coming after me for talking to you?"

Gabby scoffed. "I don't think you have to worry about him. Besides, he doesn't own me, and no man ever will." She noticed Landon raised his eyebrows, and she silently cursed herself for being so defensive. "I'm sorry, that came off crass. Do I still have feelings for Parker? yes. We dated for five years, and despite his silence, I'm not one to toss aside that much investment of time. Will he ever hold a place in my life again? I don't think so. I'm feeling a lot of things right now," she said, turning him to face her. "I feel like you're someone I'd like to get to know."

"I can accept those terms," Landon said, his finger trailing the strand of hair back behind her ear.

Awkward silence lingered before Landon dropped his arm to his side and tapped the railing with his other hand. "So, have you lived here all your life?"

Gabby smiled and held up her index finger. "No way. It's your turn. You tell me all your secrets. Or at least the one that brought you away from sand and surf to the mountains of Nano Springs."

Landon's hands brushed against his pants as he attempted to wipe the sweat from them. He wanted to share with her. She made it easy. Conversations like these didn't happen every day. Even with his close friend Brian, they were few and far between. He needed to talk about it. To get it out may help put the incident behind him. Would she turn and run? There was so much about his relationship with Jessica that lingered in his mind like a blind spot. Maybe because he'd spent the past three months blocking out the horror that his life had become.

"Goodness, look at the sweat across your brow. It's practically glistening in the light of the streetlamp. You don't have to say anything you don't want to. We can talk about the weather or what you hope to see while you're in town." Gabby placed her hand on his arm, and like a cloud dissipating in the air, all the anxiety melted away.

"Thank you. I want to tell you. There's this force in the universe that makes me want to tell you every detail. I fear that though, because I don't know what's going on here. I don't understand why I'm so drawn to you."

Traffic on the street on either side of the park passed with light thumps of tires on the pavement. A horn honked in the distance. A couple walked along the path, though they didn't pay him or Gabby any attention. They were lost in deep conversation, though theirs seemed much less intense.

"I feel the same way. We don't have to rush anything unless you're leaving tomorrow. Even then, this is nothing more right now than conversation. Company for the evening before I need to get back to my job and you to whatever you need to do." Gabby motioned for them to walk. "There's a bench up ahead. I need to get off my feet. But if you're up for it, I'd love to stay a little longer."

The warm temperature welcomed a cool breeze, the perfect weather. If he was going to talk about his past, he needed to be moving. He told her as much. When she looped her arm through his and leaned into him, the words fell from his mouth.

Landon arrived home three months earlier from work at his usual time: five o'clock. His construction firm landed a new deal and with it came a very expensive bottle of wine. Before he climbed from his SUV, he reached into the backseat to grab the bottle of sparkling grape juice. The wine substitute was a favorite of Jessica's now that she was carrying their child. He'd stepped out of the car and that's when everything exploded, his house and his life. The fire from the home jumped over to the car that thankfully he was thrown away from when the house went up. Other than the shattered pieces of his heart, his leg was the only thing physically that suffered. A second-degree burn ran up his right leg to his calf. On extremely hot days, it throbbed like a reminder of the heat from that day.

"Oh my God."

Landon opened his eyes and realized they'd stopped close to where they started walking. So lost in the memory, he hadn't realized they didn't make it far. Gabby gripped his arm, tears threatening to roll down her face. Damnit, he'd made her cry.

"I'm sorry. That's a little much for a first date—or meeting, huh? I didn't mean to upset you."

Gabby swiped a tear that escaped from her eye. "I'm sitting here whining over a boyfriend who ditched me and stopped calling while you're over here suffering. Understanding now see why you looked like you wanted to throw up earlier. I'm so sorry for asking you to share that."

Landon had no regrets. Except maybe not tell his story to the first woman he found attractive within an hour after they met. Who does that?

The story didn't end there, but he thought saying anything else wouldn't make Gabby feel any better. If he even saw her after tonight, he'd count himself lucky.

Without a word, he pulled her forward, and they began walking around the trail. Once they completed a full circle, they'd shared everything from Gabby's hesitation about her best friend's new relationship, to Landon's friendship with Brian, the business partner he left in California. As night turned into the next day, Landon walked Gabby to her car.

"Gabby, thank you for listening to me ramble." He raised her hand to his lips and softly pressed them against her skin.

"Such the gentleman. I'm glad Christina made me come out. I almost forgot about her." Gabby laughed and unlocked the door. "I'm sure my phone has a ton of missed messages."

Her words lingered in the silence that had become early morning. Unsure of what to say; did he invite her on a real date? Say goodbye and thank God for the best night since the accident?

"Would you like to come to the Inn for dinner tomorrow night? My guests are leaving in the morning, and I usually make a light dinner anyway." Gabby lowered herself behind the wheel and gazed up at him, awaiting his response.

How could he say no? "I'd love to."

They said goodnight, and he shut the door as she turned the car on and shifted in reverse. He laid his heart open, and she didn't run or crush him. Landon felt heard for the first time since that day, but she didn't make him feel like he was the saddest man on earth. Maybe Nano Springs would help him heal. If she'll let him, he'd love to help her heal too.

Chapter Four

Gabby tried to tell herself she shouldn't have invited Landon to dinner, but it wasn't like she was cheating on Parker. For all she knew, Parker moved on a month ago. That didn't give her an excuse to frolic around with the first man that paid attention to her. But it also didn't mean she shouldn't enjoy a friendly conversation when it came around. *She wasn't doing anything wrong.* That's the five words she kept repeating to herself as she unloaded the groceries from the car the next morning.

Landon would be there in six hours, and she wanted to be ready. He'd bared his soul to her and, for reasons she couldn't explain, even to herself, she felt connected to him. They didn't get into the aftermath of the accident; she hadn't wanted to question him further. Not after seeing the pain that crossed his face when he was in the middle of his story. There was more to it. She knew he'd left some things out, but it wasn't her place to push. He didn't owe her anything.

The cellphone in her back pocket chirped with a new notification. *Christina.* It surprised her that Christina hadn't shown up on her doorstep in the middle of the night. When she got home, the last thing she wanted was to spend hours on the phone analyzing their conversation with her. It was bad enough it took her hours to fall asleep as she played out every scenario that could happen on her own.

Girl. I'm on my way over. I can't believe what I'm hearing.

Great. Jamie must have told Christina about her leaving the bar with Landon. Gabby ignored the text. There was no use responding. Instead, she focused on putting away the groceries and prepping the dinner. Last night's guests checked out after breakfast, and the next reservations for the evening had been cancelled. Losing a night of business never felt good, but at least she could collect the cancellation fee. Besides, guests at the inn meant little privacy for her own company.

Christina burst through the front door, offering her favorite iced coffee from a shop in town. Gabby took it and placed it beside her in front of the cutting board.

Her friend pulled her hair back with a fabric headband, though everything else about her seemed flustered. The dress she wore reached her ankles. Gabby tried to hide her smile at the way her friend was trying to appease Jacob's mother. When she and Parker dated, Gabby refused to change what she wore or anything about herself. Scarlett loved modesty and what Gabby called "uppity" around those in town. People talked either because they respected you, or they thought low of you. Scarlett hated negativity. Gabby hoped Christina wouldn't change herself too much for the woman.

The carrots for the stew that night were uncut on the cutting board. A knife lingered in the air, poised to cut, when Gabby heard the door. She placed the knife down and took a deep breath. She'd been rehearsing what to say since she got Christina's text.

"Hey, Chris. How's your mom?"

Christina shook her head, "No ma'am, we're not going there." She made a beeline for the fridge.

She must have sensed the hurt look on Gabby's face because she turned around and huffed. "Mom is fine. She's just a little out of touch these days and forgets things. I got her settled and then went to Jacob's for the night. Now, let's talk about you."

"You're acting like the world just shifted out of orbit. This can't be about what I think it's about."

Gabby noticed the rolled-up magazine under her arm as she climbed onto the barstool on the opposite side of the counter. "You mean the hot guy? Yeah, it's a little about him." Christina popped the cap off the soda and took a drink before continuing.

"Okay." Gabby hesitated to add anything else. The knife blade sliced through the vegetables as she waited.

Christina plopped the magazine open on the counter before them. "I don't want to upset you. This came out today. I saw it online first in a news story and found the magazine at the grocery store. I'm so sorry, babe."

The glossy pages caught the sunlight coming in from the big kitchen window. On the left side were a bunch of words Gabby didn't bother to read. A chill swept through her body as she ran her eyes over the half page glossy image of Parker with a red-haired woman. Not a big deal, since she knew he had a love interest in the show. The caption caused her hands to tremble and her heart to ache, a bruised organ not quite healed. Parker was kissing the woman who, according to the headline, was not another actress, but the show's executive associate.

Gabby shoved the magazine away. Her hair fell into her eyes, and she aggressively shoved it over off her forehead. So, this was what she meant to him. Parker knew that he'd be photographed. Not only was he cheating on her, but he was being open about it. The level of disrespect was so overwhelming she had to place her head between her legs before she passed out.

"Whoa. I didn't think it would affect you this much. I shouldn't have said anything." Christina walked around the counter and rubbed her hand over her back a few times before making Gabby stand and face her. "I may be with his brother, but I can still support you and hate him. You don't deserve this."

She didn't deserve it, but maybe this was exactly the closure she needed to move on. To distract herself from the magazine, she moved behind the counter and finished preparing the stew. Regardless of the shock she felt now from this news, a dinner guest would arrive expecting dinner, and she didn't want to disappoint.

Tap Tap Tap. Gabby turned to look over her shoulder to see Christina's worried expression as her fingernail clicked on the counter. "Want to talk about it?"

The last thing Gabby wanted to do was talk about how the love of her life left her. He didn't just leave her; he exited the relationship stage right and ruined everything. The thought of cancelling the evening with Landon crossed her mind a time or two. When she glanced at the magazine again, she decided to keep her dinner plans. Why should she sit at home crying over a lost relationship when he was out creating a new one before telling her anything? No, tonight she'd have fun.

"What's to talk about?" she asked, pouring the freshly chopped vegetables into the beef broth on the stove. "It's clear he moved on. I can't even ask him to make sure because he's cut off all contact. You know I don't like to jump to conclusions without checking first. What am I supposed it do?"

Christina sighed and planted herself on the barstool again. She leaned over the counter and shrugged her shoulders. "I don't know what you should do, but I am here to talk. Tell me about Dreamy Eyes then."

Shattered Yesterdays

Gabby wasn't ready to share Landon with Christina, but she didn't hesitate to go into detail about their conversation. The story he told about his former girlfriend was truly heartbreaking and even had tough as nails Christina in near tears. To lose someone you love that way was unthinkable. At least if Gabby insisted on closure from Parker, all she needed to do was fly to L.A. and demand him to tell her to her face he was done.

Christina listened and reacted in all the right places like a good friend, should but didn't ask all the questions that ran through Gabby's own head. Why did the house explode? How did the explosion happen? Landon mentioned Jessica was pregnant, so not only did he lose a loved one, but a baby. Gabby finished the stew and placed the lid on the pot. She hoped tonight they could get to know each other better. Gabby welcomed new friendships as a naturally social person, and she couldn't lie to herself, he was hot.

Once the sun sank below the clouds, Christina said goodbye and left Gabby to dress for Landon's arrival. Tonight she chose another dress, this one powder blue with a slit up the side, so when she sat down it showed a little skin. She wasn't expecting anything, but damn, a woman had needs. With dinner done and smelling delicious, the table set with the fancy plates; she watched Landon pull around and park on the circular drive. Time to put Parker out of her mind and focus on healing a broken heart by letting someone else fit the pieces back into place.

Landon adjusted his gray tie and checked his hair in the rearview mirror. He'd taken care this evening of his appearance to show Gabby he could clean up nicely when needed. The pressed khaki pants and the crisp white dress shirt clung to his sturdy frame. He took a deep breath and slid from the car he'd rented when he got to town. Landon hadn't chosen a return date to San Fransisco, though if he was honest with himself, he never wanted to return. Loose ends needed to be taken care of, but for tonight, that could wait. Nano Springs had a way of making him feel at home. Gabby made things even better, but the atmosphere alone drew him in like a moth to a flame.

The paper crinkled under his fingertips as he gripped the flowers he'd bought from Sally's Flower Shop next to the apartment. The long stem lilies gave off a sweet aroma that tickled his nose. His hands shook as he reached up and gave a few gentle knocks on the royal blue door. Sweat threatened to drip down the back of his neck, though the temperature outside was not even close to being too hot. His nerves liked to get the best of him when it came to beautiful women.

Gabby opened the door and took his breath away. She'd swept her brown hair up in a clip, with a few pieces hanging loose down the back of her neck. He loved the way she didn't feel the need to wear too much make-up, only enough to highlight her best features. Her eyes. Green with specks of brown. The dress she wore clung to her hips and didn't go any further than her knees. Everything his eyes saw made him want to get to know her so much more.

"Hi," she said, her smile stretching across her face. "Come on in." She stepped aside to let him walk in and he couldn't take his eyes off of her.

"Thanks for having me. Whatever's for dinner smells fantastic."

She closed the door and gestured for him to follow her. "Beef Stew. My dad taught me the family recipe when I was ten years old. It's become a staple in my life."

The dining room was quaint, with a large farmhouse style table in the center of the room. Benches for sitting were on either side and a ruby cloth lay over the table. A three light chandelier hung at the center, giving off enough light in the room to set its own romantic hue. It was the perfect setup for a nice quiet dinner together, though only one end of the table was set with dishes.

Conversation at dinner lowered Landon's tension that wove through the muscles in his shoulders. He could feel himself relax as he listened to how she came to run the Inn. The way her eyes lit up as she talked about the improvements she wanted to make to the place made him eager to see them come to fruition. Her energy was as radiant as the sparkle in her eyes. Landon wanted to tell her he'd be around to help with any remodeling or minor things that needed to be done. But he couldn't.

As they scooped out the ice-cream from the porcelain dishes, he admitted the hardest thing to her. "I'm leaving to go back to San Francisco in the morning." As she spoke of her own plans, he mentally began making his own.

"Oh," she said, her eyes focused on her spoon. "That's too bad."

"I know. I was enjoying our time together. But I need to figure things out and at the very least tie up some loose ends."

Brian warned him about telling Gabby this when Landon shared her story with his friend. No matter when he left Nano Springs, it would affect her. Brian McLane was his best friend and business partner. It was because of him that Landon could break away and get out of California. Brian believed telling Gabby would be disastrous, considering how her boyfriend left things. Landon scoffed at him earlier, but a hint of sadness that passed over Gabby's face when he said he was going back to California told him how it affected her. Heartbreak was easy to read when you've been through it yourself.

"Gabby, I've loved my time here. Not only because of the bright spot you've brought to my life in the last twenty-four hours, but this town. There's something magical about it." He reached for her hand across the table and stroked the back of it with his thumb. "I don't want to leave." Landon knew promises at this stage of their friendship meant nothing, especially since Parker had broken her trust. He had to try. "I have already made a list of things to do once I get home, and some of them are already in motion. I've also rented the apartment I'm staying in for three more months. The owner said if I paid upfront, she'd be sure not to rent it and credit me when he returns. I'll be back, Gabby. I won't promise, because promises are so fragile right now, but I won't be away long."

He waited. She was silent for so long; he wondered what was going through her mind. When he noticed a tear rolling down her cheek, he stood and pulled her into his arms. "I'm sorry I made you cry."

"Don't be. These are happy tears. I got news today about Parker and I think it's just made me a little more sensitive than I should be," she explained. Gabby assured him she didn't want to let what Parker did to her ruin any chances of moving on. Maybe it was premature, but she was going to trust him. He'd do everything in his power to not break that trust.

They spent the rest of the evening cuddled on the couch, talking about everything but their pasts. Gabby told him more about the town and the big events of the year, and Landon shared with him the idea of taking the construction business and expanding.

When the clock on the mantle by the fireplace struck midnight, Gabby turned and took his glass of wine he'd been nursing and placed it on the table.

"I rarely do this on the first date. But, since it's the second date and nothing has to come from it, would you like to stay the night?"

Landon didn't know what to say, so he simply nodded his

head and waited for her to make a move. Was it too soon? No. They were consenting adults, right? The indecision disappeared as quickly as it came when Gabby reached for his hand.

She leaned down to blow out the candles and led him from the room. They made it to her bedroom a few moments later. Once inside, he let her take control. Darkness swarmed his vision as he closed his eyes to let the things cover his senses completely.

Chapter Five

Every time Parker picked up the phone, something came up and he couldn't bring himself to dial her number. Time passed so quickly with the T.V. show, filming, and the parties after work. Before he knew it, two months passed since he last saw Gabby's beautiful face. He regretted the distance he'd put between them. Now, with the photographers shooting promotional spots, Parker doubted Gabby would ever forgive him.

The photograph with him and Sasha really put a mark on his card; not only did it look bad, but was posted in every celebrity magazine. Sasha told him to brush it off, that Gabby would understand. One thing Gabby could never forgive him for would be his second night in town. Sasha invited him over to celebrate his official acceptance of the role he'd auditioned for. Parker thought the party meant more than the two of them, but Sasha had other plans. When he kissed her, he told himself Gabby would forgive him. When he pulled Sasha's bra off with his teeth, he knew he was pushing the limits. But it was when Sasha lowered herself over his bare skin that pushed the thought of Gabby completely from his mind.

For weeks he'd paced the length of his room at the house rented by the producers. They'd given him the suite as part of his contract. The home was located a few miles from the set, and it made it easier to have him nearby. Many nights, he searched his mind for ways to convince Gabby that he still loved her. Sasha had stayed away at his request, only to talk business when they needed to get together.

Two months after he arrived in L.A., Parker dialed a number and held his breath.

"Hello?"

"Jacob, man, it's me. How are ya?" Parker coughed to clear his voice. "I'm sorry I haven't called sooner. Just been so busy, man."

"Parker?"

Parker heard whispering in the background. A female voice that sounded very much like Christina chimed in. Gabby's best friend would show no mercy. Better to just play it cool and keep the Sasha thing to himself. After a few moments of shuffling, Jacob came back on the line.

"Sorry, was a little busy myself."

"Yeah. So. How's things going?" Parker sat on his bed, propped against a plush white pillow. The big window overlooked the backyard that dropped off a cliff. The views were enough to not miss Vermont. Though he wished he could share them with Gabby.

"We're all good here, man. Kind of wondering what the hell is wrong with you, though," Jacob said, not holding back the anger in his voice.

Parker hung his head. "I know. I have a lot of explaining to do."

"I think you lost her, Parker."

He appreciated Jacob not sugar coating anything, but the words still hurt. Surely Gabby would forgive him. He still had four months left on his promise. Had she already written him off?

"Gabby saw the photo. How could you be so stupid?"

Damn the paparazzi. "That—was just a photo op," he said, stuttering over his words. "She knew I'd have to kiss people out here. It's part of the job."

Jacob sighed. Even his brother didn't have faith in him anymore. "Parker, that woman wasn't a co-star. Pretty sure you're not supposed to be kissing executive assistants."

"Yeah, so it looks bad. Do you really think she won't forgive me for that?"

Jacob was silent.

"Jacob? You still there?"

"Parker, I shouldn't be telling you this."

Parker stared out the window and watched an eagle swoop into a nearby tree, waiting for the other shoe to drop right on top of his heart.

"I think she's moving on now. I mean, it's new, but if you come home soon, there may be a chance to save your relationship."

Parker exhaled a breath he'd been holding in. "I can't just drop everything and come back there. The plan was to come back in four months and reevaluate things, assuming filming is done for this season. The pilot was picked up two weeks ago, so if all goes well, there could be more seasons of the show. I told Gabby this."

He could hear the disappointment in Jacob's voice. "Have fun, Parker. Might as well at this point. You could have at least called her. Wasn't that the deal?"

"Like I said, things are just so busy here. It moves much faster than Vermont."

He heard the disappointment dripping from his brother's voice, "you called me, but you haven't called her."

"I know, but—," Parker started.

The click was loud against his ear. He stared at the phone in his hand, the other end having gone dead. Parker didn't have long to linger in his feelings before he was no longer alone. Sasha wandered into the room with a pouty lip. Was she eavesdropping? He quickly learned secrets weren't kept in this profession. Instead of scolding her, Parker smiled and stood to greet her.

"Sorry. I kind of overheard the end of your conversation. Are you okay?"

Parker nodded, placing the phone on the bed. "I'll be fine." He'd have to snuff out the slow burn that overcame his heart, but he'd be fine.

Gabby couldn't contain her excitement anymore. Landon would be in Nano Springs by the end of the day. They'd stayed in touch from the moment he left until he hopped on the plane to return to Vermont. He'd kept his promise. It meant more to her than he'd ever know, but she planned to do whatever she needed to show him.

The late night phone calls, whispering under the blankets, and daily text messages were almost enough for her to forget the loss of Parker. Gabby and Landon even talked about the last night they were together, the boldness she'd never had with a man. Gabby had only ever been with one person until that night.

The sheets were washed and new ones placed on the beds in each of the five guest rooms. Once the Inn was cleaned and ready for check-ins later that afternoon, she set about fixing her hair and finding something to wear. The nausea came and went, though she brushed it off at the excitement of Landon's arrival. Jacob and Christina were coming over for a BBQ the next day so they could get to know the new man in her life. Parker was never a distant thought; in fact, she thought of him off and on over the last month. Jacob told her of the phone call he had with him, and his excuse for not being able to come home or even call.

Jacob told him about Landon, though indirectly, and it annoyed her, but what hurt the most was Parker's carelessness about losing her. Jacob gave him the perfect chance to come home and reunite with her, but he refused. That told her either he didn't care and thought she wouldn't leave him for someone else, or he'd already moved on with the assistant. Bottom line: he didn't care.

If Landon wanted to be with her, what's a little harm in getting to know him better? During their time a part, Landon told her more about his relationship with Jessica. Gabby wanted to know about the woman that caused him so much hurt, though at one time, held his heart. Their story was tragic; from the suicide note Jessica left in the mailbox that fateful day, to the reason she cut the gas line and lit the match. It wasn't about Landon at all, but about her own inner demons.

After he shared the rest of the story about Jessica's death, she did her own research online. Everything was there; the investigation, the stories from the neighbors, and the exoneration of the fiancé left fatherless. Gabby wanted to hold him after that. There would be plenty of time for comfort.

As the morning wore on, Gabby couldn't shake the upset stomach. The perks of living in a small town meant being able to get a doctor's appointment easily. Gabby gathered her purse just before lunch and made her way into town. Christina offered to meet her there and grab lunch once she was done.

· · ·

Dr. Matthis's office was the only family health clinic in a fifty-mile radius, with the hospital being twenty minutes outside of town. Having the same doctor since she was a child really helped with any medical issues that arose. Thankfully she didn't have any of those. The once young man now had a head full of gray hair and friendly wrinkles at the corner of his eyes. His son would take over the business in a few years, but for now, Gabby scheduled her appointments with Dr. Matthis.

The sound of traffic hummed around her as she walked down the sidewalk to the office. Main street had family-owned businesses lining the whole strip. Their own kind of Vegas without the lights, excessive noise, and crime. Summer was ending soon and Gabby loved the changing of the leaves that would come in the next few weeks.

Christina stayed as busy as Gabby these days with her work at the dispatch office. The Nano Springs Police and Fire Departments were housed in one building down the road. While they weren't as active as the bigger cities, it didn't stop people from calling about every little thing. Christina told her stories about the silliest calls during their once-a-week mandatory friendship meeting. A day each week where they made time for each other, no matter what.

The two were friends before Gabby met Parker, but immediately grew a liking for the Warrick boys. Parker apparently wanted to get the hell out of town, though Jacob was happy joining the fire department and putting down roots. Gabby tried not to be jealous of the way life was laying out for her friend, but on days when she still missed Parker, she couldn't keep the sadness away.

Dr. Matthis's clinic sat between a used bookstore and the pet shop. A small brick building that had changed little over the years. The specially made wooden sign hung over the door that read the doctor's name and the address; a staple in the community for over twenty years. It had become detached on one end, causing Gabby to duck cautiously under it as she opened the matching wooden door.

The office was empty. Thankfully, the last thing Gabby wanted was someone else coming up to her and asking about Parker. She didn't know what to tell them, and frankly; it hurt to talk about him. She'd been humoring the idea of flying out to L.A. and facing him, but she didn't want to seem crazy girl-friend stalker-ish. Christina said she'd come with her, as she had a few choice words for him, but Gabby brushed the idea aside.

"Hey there, Miss Gabby," the receptionist said politely. Lori greeted everyone with so much kindness you could catch a cavity with her sweetness. A long-time employee of Dr. Matthis's, she was always a bright spot at each doctor visit.

"Hey, Lori. I'm here for my appointment," Gabby said, handing the middle-aged woman her insurance card.

"I'll get you checked in shortly. Dr. Matthis is just getting back from lunch."

Gabby tucked her card back into her wallet and found a seat in the waiting room. Before she could open the magazine on a nearby table, Christina stepped through the door.

"Are you okay? Have you gotten sick again?"

Gabby shook her head. "It's nothing serious. Probably a stomach bug."

They chatted about work and other happenings around town until the nurse called Gabby back to the exam room. Christina opted to wait in the waiting room. They were best friends, but some things were personal. Besides, if there was anything to tell, Gabby would share it with her first.

The nurse took her through a standard checkup: temperature, weight, height, and blood pressure. When she left the room, Gabby clutched her stomach and really thought about how to address Parker's absence. With Landon coming to Nano

Springs to stay, at least for a few months, Gabby needed to know if she and Parker were through or not. Could she really close the door on the last five years of her relationship?

You slept with the man who is moving here to be closer to you. The door is pretty much already shut. She had to decide if the door would stay closed.

Before she could dwell on the issue any further, Dr. Matthis gave a gentle knock on the door before poking his head in the room. Once he had her symptoms and offered a reassuring pat on the hand, he ordered some tests and left the room. When the door closed behind him, Gabby dabbed the sweat that formed on her forehead.

"Gabby, you okay, hon?" Christina's voice echoed in her ears. Gabby gripped the bed and eased herself into a fetal position.

"How did I not think about that?" she whispered to herself.

"About what? What did the doctor say?"

What had she done? Of all the stupid mistakes she could have made at this stage of her life. Gabby buried her face in her hands and sobbed.

"He's ordering a pregnancy test," she cried, sobbing after each word.

She heard Christina let out a vast sigh as her hand rubbed her back. Soothing tones of comfort and reassurance poured from her mouth, but nothing could calm Gabby at this point. Pregnant? A mom? No. She couldn't be.

"Gabby, it's just a test. A precaution. Let's wait until we get the results before we get ourselves worked up over it."

Christina was right. That was the reason she brought her levelheaded friend with her to the doctor to begin with, to calm her down. But, pregnant? She didn't even let the thought cross her mind. Gabby took her birth control like clockwork, it was ingrained into her daily regime.

The clinic had its own lab at the back of the building. A part of the old way of medicine that Dr. Matthis hadn't wanted to let go of. Nowadays, you had to go to a separate clinic to get bloodwork or other lab tests done. Gabby appreciated the simplicity of a one-stop shop. Once she'd given what felt like a pint of blood, and a deposit in a cup, they left the clinic. Lunch was no longer something Gabby was interested in, so she had Christina follow her to the Inn.

Because the clinic serviced such a small town, it didn't take long before the results were in. Gabby dropped the phone on the desk a few hours after her appointment.

She was pregnant.

Parker smiled and leaned against the fake living room on the set of his show. His director gave the news that the network loved the show and pleased with the cast. Life was good. He had the rest of the day off and Sasha left him to wander the set on his own. She wanted to celebrate with dinner that evening at the hottest place in town but, needed her nails to reflect the success of the show. Whatever that meant. Parker never understood why women felt the need to do so much extra to themselves.

He had a few hours to kill and not enough time to go back to the condo he shared with Sasha. They'd moved in together the week before, and so far, it was the perfect setup. Jacob made it clear Gabby was moving on and if he didn't lie to himself, he'd have to admit the screw ups he'd caused over the last two months meant he should move on too. Gabby wouldn't want him after she found out what he'd done.

Parker grabbed his bag from the trailer and stepped onto the street outside the studio. In the glare of the California sun, he couldn't believe his eyes. Was that Gabby? She stood across the street, a small carry-on bag gripped in one hand, and her other slowly pulling off her sunglasses. She wore a flowing floral dress that reached her knees. Those sexy legs that used to wrap themselves around him whenever they were intimately together. He'd missed her. He couldn't deny that. Why was she here?

It was too much to hope she'd changed her mind. Besides, her suitcase was too small to hold everything she owned. He lifted his hand and smiled as he stepped toward her. Before he could stop himself, he rushed to her side of the street and pulled her into his arms. The tears that dripped from her face landed on his baby blue golf shirt, leaving stains that would evaporate in the California sun. She still smelled of lilacs and lavender, like he remembered.

"I can't believe you're here."

She pushed herself from his arms and stepped backwards. "I came to see if you could tell me to my face why you broke the biggest promise you'd ever made to me."

The woman didn't waste any time, Parker thought.

Suddenly, a flash of red tugged his gaze away from her. Sasha pulled up to the curb in her red mustang. "Hey babe, I finished early. Need a lift home?"

Parker cringed.

"Well. Look at what we have here," Gabby said, fresh tears trailing down her cheeks. "Closure."

Parker fumbled over his words, but didn't stop her from storming down the street.

Chapter Six

G abby sobbed the entire way to the airport. The Uber driver who picked her up three blocks from where she left Parker almost didn't want to take her on. A woman sobbing, mascara painting her cheeks black, wasn't the ideal customer. Now that she was in the air on the most expensive last-minute flight available, Gabby dried her eyes and considered her options. When the news of her pregnancy settled in, she threw an overnight change of clothes in the carry-on and found a flight to L.A.

She left Christina flustered, but she agreed to cover the Inn for a few days. Little did Gabby know at the time her trip would end so soon. Gabby couldn't believe Parker had really moved on. A part of her knew not to read too much into a magazine article. News these days was nothing but people's opinions anyway; a believe at your own risk. Especially with Hollywood and the disaster that came out of that town. But she wanted to give him the benefit of the doubt.

No. She should have trusted her gut and saved herself a couple thousand dollars in airfare. She'd need that money in the months to come as she prepared for the baby. A baby? Twenty-six seemed old to be starting a family, but she wasn't ready. Well, ready or not, the baby was coming. Gabby dropped the tray table onto her lap. She pulled her cell phone from her pocket and flipped it over to the wi-fi calling mode.

Landon arrived at the Burlington airport an hour before her flight was to land from L.A. They weren't planning to meet up again until the next day, but Gabby needed to cancel. She wasn't ready to face the greatest guy who'd walked into her life in years, at least not yet. A quick text that it would be a few days until she'd be free, allowed her a little breathing room.

By the time she arrived at the Inn eight hours later, the place was pitch dark with a small lamp on the desk at the entry-way. Christina met her on the porch and took her bag from her. The weight of her friends' arms around her shoulders nearly made the tears fall again.

"Let's go inside." Gabby grabbed her bag and stepped into the hallway. The guests who checked in shortly after she left were due to check out in four hours. They'd only needed a stopover night and because of the slow season, Gabby allowed it. Usually there was a two-night minimum. The couple were older and on their way to meet their grand-baby the next day. Thinking of them now reminded Gabby to make plans to have her own parents over that evening. It was time to change their lives, too.

Gabby said goodbye to Christina and made her way up to her bedroom. She tip-toed past the second level and the guest rooms there. Footsteps caused the floor to groan, which told her the couple were already awake. She placed her bag in her room and set about making breakfast in the kitchen downstairs. Maybe they'd leave sooner and she'd have time for a quick nap.

The sun peaked over the mountain, casting a dewy haze over the lake as she placed fresh blueberry muffins, sliced fruit, and a steaming pot of coffee on the table. Who needed sleep, right? Thankfully, the guests checking out were the last reservations for the week. The calendar was blacked out for the month before the annual Labor Day Festivities.

This year, the Inn was hosting a community cook-out in the backyard near the lake. There would be fireworks and a lot of food, music to fit any genre style, and even a dance floor. Each year, a different business got the chance to showcase their property and host the festivities. This was an important event this year because if things went well, she knew the owners would be more open to handing over the lease of the Inn sooner.

Gabby spent the morning greeting her guests, making small talk, and then cleaning their room once they checked out. It was almost therapeutic because it allowed her to get lost in her thoughts, and boy did she have a lot of those. Her relationship with Parker was over, at least romantically. If she were honest with herself, she wasn't sure who fathered her baby. Thoughts such as these nearly chased her under the covers in her third-floor bedroom. How could she be so stupid? The town would have a field day, but most wouldn't blame her. She'd heard the mumblings over the last month and people weren't too forgiving of Parker for leaving her. Gabby nearly laughed at the comments some were saying, as if her life were a soap opera. The Days of Gabby Lawson's Life. What a hoot.

As the hours passed, Gabby stopped looking at her phone. A small part of her still thought Parker would call or text, begging for forgiveness. But she was fooling herself. He'd moved on, and she needed to accept that. Just as she put her phone away for the last time, she spotted her parents' car rolling into the driveway. They parked under the oak tree and clasps their hands together as they met at the rear of the car.

Gabby wanted that. She wanted marriage and a husband who would think about her happiness, or at least be considerate of how sudden life changes made her feel. That was what both-

ered her the most; one day they were living their best lives and
the next he was gone. She brushed aside the resentment
building in her chest and opened the screen door for her
parents.

"Hey, Mom. Dad."

She ushered them to the back porch overlooking the lake,
where a tray of lemonade and an assortment of cheeses waited
for them. To tell them now, or let them fill their stomachs first?
She wasn't sure. Gabby's mother sat in the white rocking chair
and offered her a smile so large Gabby could see every one of
her teeth.

"So. When's the due date?"

Gabby sighed as she dropped into the chair beside her
father. She should have known someone wouldn't be able to
mind their business. She'd be angrier if she didn't thrive on the
gossip too, though she didn't like it as much when it was
centered towards her.

"Let me guess, Christina?"

"No, Susan." Gabby's father said, happily reaching for a
slice of goat cheese.

Susan was the server at Leon's on Main Street. She served
burgers and fish baskets on Friday nights. How on earth did she
know about her pregnancy?

"Oh, no!" Gabby moaned. Her hands covered her face as
she leaned back in the chair. If Susan knew, then it wouldn't be
long before Landon found out as well. If he didn't know already.

"Honey, it's okay." Gabby felt her mother's hand on her
knee. The woman didn't know the mess she'd gotten herself
into.

"Mom, there's something else I need to tell you."

A knock echoed through the house and onto the porch.
She wasn't expecting anyone, and she'd told Christina her
parents would be visiting. "Who could that be?" Gabby stood.

The side door opened onto the porch and out stepped Landon.

Gabby had forgotten how handsome he was, and despite the concerned expression on his face, she still blushed whenever he was close. He wore a pair of blue jean pants and a flannel shirt, rolled up at the forearms. Landon looked every bit like a local.

"I'm sorry to interrupt. I didn't realize you'd have company." He backed away, but Gabby's dad came forward and stopped him.

"Not an interruption at all. You must be Landon."

Gabby rolled her eyes. Good Lord, there were no secrets in Nano Springs. "How do you know about Landon?"

Gabby's mother laughed. "Darling, we've lived here for forty years. You know a newcomer doesn't stick around here without us knowing about him. Especially if he's seen chatting up our daughter."

Jamie, from the bar. It had to be him. The blabbermouth. Not being able to have alcohol for the next eight months was looking more inviting. Though a stiff drink would do her good. Gabby flipped her hair over her head and twirled it up in a bun. The hair tie on her wrist held her hair up as she contemplated how to handle the issues that lay before her. Who to address first? Landon, who looked like he'd swallowed a bee, or her parents who were fawning over the poor man like he was a juicy beefsteak.

"Oh God," she said, rocking back and forth on her heels. "I think I'm going to be sick."

Gabby's mother waved her hand in the air as she stepped towards Landon. "Oh, it's fine sweetie. You'll get used to it and the sickness will pass soon."

"Mother!" Gabby cried.

She wasn't paying attention. Both of her parents were standing in front of Landon, smiling. "We've heard so much about you, young man," her father said. "I'm Gabby's father, Andy, and this here is her mother, Claire."

Landon pleaded with her with his eyes, as if he were begging for an escape. Gabby couldn't leave him in her parent's clutches. "Let's all sit down. For crying out loud, let the man breathe."

Once everyone settled in their seats, and held a fresh glass of lemonade, Gabby cleared her throat. "Well. That's enough excitement for me for one lifetime." She laughed nervously as she scanned her eyes over her three guests. "Where do I begin?"

Gabby didn't want to talk about the pregnancy with Landon yet, especially at the same time as her parents. He looked scared and her parents acted like they were given the greatest gift in the world. Sure, a baby meant different things to different people; but even she wasn't sure how she felt about being a mother yet. The last twenty-four hours were a whirlwind of shock, fear, disappointment, and embarrassment. Not adjectives she wanted her baby to know about when they shared stories of its arrival.

Gabby's father rescued her as he's always done. "Your mom and I won't hang around long. We're so happy about this news. While I know it's a shock, just remember, a baby is a blessing. We'll support you no matter what, but know that this baby won't lack for love." The man always had a way of swiping a hand over anything of distress and smoothing out even the roughest edges. "Now, Claire, finish your lemonade so we can give these kids some space."

When they drained the last drops from their glasses, Gabby reminded them of the fireworks display they would oversee for the festival. Her mother pulled her into the warmest of hugs and assured her everything was ready to go. "So much to celebrate," she squealed, just a little too loudly in Gabby's ear.

Silence hung over the porch once her parents left. Even the

crickets in the evening air were quiet, as if ready to sing the melody of whatever unfolded in the minutes to come. Gabby faced Landon and shrugged her shoulders. What was there to say? Besides, she was sorry for bringing this into their lives. Like a floodgate escaping a dam, the questions and insecurities flooded her mind. Who was the father? Had their relationship ended before it could even begin?

Before she opened her mouth to ask every question assaulting her mind, he opened his arms and welcomed her into the folds. Like a magnet to metal, she stepped into him and allowed his kindness to settle around her. She didn't know the answers, but for now, he was hers.

Landon held Gabby for a while before she backed away and started clearing the table. He helped carry in the glasses and placed them in the dishwasher. He didn't pressure her to talk. It didn't take a genius to see she was not only tired, but mentally spent. When he overhead Susan at the diner questioning if Parker knew about the baby, he didn't hesitate to drive to the Inn. The need to see her, to ask, was the gossip true overrode his respectful nature. Thankfully, the whole family seemed to be of understanding minds. Her parents were a breath of fresh air and he loved how much support she had, not with just them, but with friends and neighbors. Landon wondered if that was why Parker was okay leaving her for months at a time. But giving that jerk a pass didn't sit well.

"I'm sorry." Gabby stared at him from across the counter. Her voice had taken a sullen tone to it. That left him worried. Did she think he would push her away because she was pregnant? He couldn't deny her pregnancy made him nervous. Women like Gabby rarely came into his life. The way she kept fighting her way forward, despite the depression that lingered in her eyes. She was incredibly strong, probably more than she saw in herself. Despite the way her body would change over the next few months, he still wanted nothing more than to get to know her better.

"Gabby, you have nothing to be sorry about." He meant it. Reaching for her hand, he pulled her to his side of the counter and rubbed her arms. Goosebumps rose on her skin. He wanted to warm her but, not crowd her.

"I feel so foolish. I can't even tell you if you're the father or not."

Wait. What did she just say?

"How far along are you?"

She hung her head, and he didn't miss the tears that dropped to the floor. "It's too early to really tell, but based on the math, I'm looking at four to eight weeks."

Now he was sorry. He forgot their one night together would put her in this position. The passion that overcame them that night, and three times more before the sun rose, made him forget protection. What use had he for it anyway? When they met, the last thing he expected was to fall into a woman's bed.

"I'm here for you, Gabby. I know we don't know each other very well, but I'd still like to change that. I'll only go if you ask me to go." He meant every word. Landon wouldn't turn his back on her. Of course, he was still processing everything, but the little he knew about Gabby only made him want to know her more. There was something real about the way she listened when he spoke, and the attention she gave to the things she cared most about. A baby was a big deal, but it shouldn't eliminate their chance at finding out if there was something between them. He'd leave it up to her to take that chance.

"Even if the baby isn't yours?" The words came from her mouth like hesitancy wrapped in a soft blanket. He didn't miss the way she swallowed, as if she were afraid of his response. He saw the hope in her eyes, the same hope he knew showed in his.

Were they crazy? To risk so much when they still knew so little about each other. Landon knew he could get hurt. The last thing he wanted to do was hurt her, but wasn't that her choice? When Jessica took her own life, even going as far as researching how to stage the accident; she always did like a good show, he vowed never to put himself in a position to love again. But Gabby changed all of that. She made him feel again, to crave more than the dark hole he'd dug himself into after Jessica.

"Would you want to get a DNA test?" He couldn't stop thinking about the idea of her carrying his baby. A second chance to be a father. It was selfish of him to not care about whose baby she was carrying, but he didn't. If they dated, fell in love, and spent the rest of their lives together, who the child's father was wouldn't change how he felt about their life. He couldn't tell her that, though. She'd go running for the hills.

Gabby ran her hand across her flat stomach. He was thankful she took care of how she responded. When she took his hand and pulled him into the sitting room, he felt the air shift around them.

"I think we should. Not that I would change my mind about you, if you're not the father, but if it is Parker's, he probably has a right to know."

Damnit. He didn't want to bring the other guy into the mix. But who was he to argue? She was right. Was it wrong of him to hope Parker wouldn't care? *Selfish bastard*, he thought of himself. "Okay. I can go with you if you'd like?"

Gabby laughed. "Well, I need you there, obviously."

Of course. How else would she be able to compare his DNA?

He was hesitant to ask. "What about tonight? Should I leave?"

When her chin dropped to her chest, he knew he wouldn't be sharing her bed.

"It's just been a long day. Longer than you can even imagine. Mind if we meet at the clinic tomorrow?"

He pulled her to him again at the door and once he got the directions to the clinic; he wished her a goodnight and headed for his car. Once he'd left the Inn behind him, he really let himself envision the possibilities of their future together.

Chapter Seven

Gabby met him at the same bridge in the park where they shared their first date. She'd come from Dr. Matthis's office and asked him to meet her there. Three weeks before, they'd entered the clinic and took their individual tests. The days passed slowly, but they tried to focus on the now and not the what ifs. Now the day had come, and the results were in. Gabby gripped the single sheet of paper in her hand. No matter how hard she tried to hide her emotions, she couldn't.

From a bag, Landon pulled two pieces of bread and offered her one. She shook her head. He tore apart the bread, tossing it into the stream below. Ducks raced towards the food in such eagerness as if they were starved of nourishment. Gabby folded and unfolded the paper until she couldn't take it any longer.

Tears streamed down her face in an even flow. She left the mascara at home today because, no matter the results, crying was inevitable. "I'm sorry." Those two words were all she needed to say. His head hung and his arms lay on the railing of the bridge. She wanted to ask him what he was thinking, but couldn't get the words out over the knot lodged in her throat.

Instead, she placed a hand on his back, hoping to convey she still wanted him.

Parker was the father, and the big-headed idiot was clueless. Gabby didn't even know how she'd tell him. Maybe Jacob or Scarlett would track down his new number and let him know. He'd since disconnected yet another cellphone, as if he didn't want to be found. She'd happily keep it that way except not telling him felt like an open wound that could get infected if she didn't do something about it.

"Gabby, this doesn't change anything for me." Landon turned to wipe away her tears. "I don't usually believe in fate, or love at first sight, or even destiny. I can't deny something pulling us together as if I was meant to find you at this point in my life."

No man had ever rolled out his emotions so openly as Landon did right then. The sincerity in his voice wasn't to be ignored. Worry etched through her mind. In a small town, people talked. It was something Gabby was familiar with, and accepted a long time ago. But did she want that for Landon? Or worse yet, her baby? How could she tell Parker without telling his family? Once his family knew, everyone would.

Moments passed as she contemplated how to address the issue. Maybe Parker didn't need to find out. If he called her again, sure, she'd tell him. Why burn a bridge before the fire was even started? Hadn't he made the choice to leave her, thus leaving his baby? It wasn't as if she hadn't tried to tell him she was pregnant. Hell, she'd flown all the way to L.A. and tracked him down.

Deep down, she knew it wasn't the same. Before she could stop herself, she told Landon how she wanted to handle it. If anyone asked, she'd politely tell them it wasn't any of their business. They'd talk either way. The real issue will be Scarlett and Jacob. Gabby didn't feel good lying to them, but she'd address it when the time came.

"This won't be easy," she said, lacing her hands in his. "Nano Springs is your stereotypical small-town and gossip flows like honey through a bear's tooth."

Landon laughed. "That's a new one." He pulled her to his chest and rested his chin on the top of her head. "Gabby, if you want me around, I will be. I don't listen to gossip, nor humor the people who spread it."

Gabby sighed and buried her face in the comfort of his neck. "We'll take things one day at a time and see how it plays out."

His body tensed, and he pulled away. "We need to let Parker know. I may not listen to gossip, but I can't have him not knowing on my conscience."

The wind picked up around them, causing ripples over the water below. In the moments of conversation, the ducks had given up on the promise of food and moved on down the stream. Gabby leaned against the metal railing and watched the leaves fall from the tree and into the water. "I, I went to see Parker in L.A. while you were gone. I didn't tell him about the baby, but he didn't give me a chance."

Gabby explained the trip and the revelation she had on the return to Vermont. The image of Parker and the changes in him since he'd driven away from her months ago still stung. Tears began pouring and before she knew it, she was sobbing. *Hormones.*

"Hey, Hey...it's okay. If you tried and it didn't work out, we can revisit telling him another time." Landon swiped his thumb across her cheek, catching a tear before he fell to the ground. "I won't leave you, Gabby. If you give me the chance, I'd love to see where this relationship goes."

"One day at a time?" she asked, running her hand through her hair. She glanced around quickly, noticing the stares from the other park goers. Great. Let the chatter begin.

"Let's get out of here." Landon grabbed her hand, and they left the park and the whispers behind.

Gabby waited anxiously on the front porch of the Inn as the sun set behind the trees that lined the driveway. The white dress she wore flowed in the early fall breeze as she watched the headlights crawl up road, and turn into one of the empty parking spots. Her nerves shook her entire body as she watched the grandmother of her baby step from the clean white car.

Scarlett Warrick didn't look a day over thirty, but as she stepped closer to the porch, the wrinkles on her forehead aged her beautifully. Gabby invited the woman to the Inn to give her the news. Landon urged her to be honest with the support system she had in Nano Springs. Christina understood, but that wasn't surprising. She insisted on being called Aunt Christina, regardless of her relationship status with Parker's brother, When Gabby mentioned Landon being in the picture, she didn't miss the hesitation in her best friend's eyes. Gabby's parents embraced the news of the baby, accepting Landon as if he were the baby's father. When she asked them why they were so understanding, they replied, "We just want you to be happy. Landon brings back the light in your eyes you lost when Parker left."

Scarlett smiled and opened her arms to wrap them around Gabby. "Hello dear, thank you for the invite. Have you heard anything from my son?"

Gabby stepped back and shook her head. "No, Ma'am, he's still unreachable."

"I swear, he's so much like his father I could scream," Scarlett said, rolling her eyes. She walked past Gabby and opened the screen door.

"I was hoping we could have tea here on the porch, if that's okay?" Gabby pointed to the white porch swing on the left side of the porch. She'd set up a tray of hot tea and cookies to share.

"Oh! How lovely. Any guests today?" Scarlett let the door bang shut and sauntered over to the swing. She tossed a pillow to the side and plopped down, causing the swing to sway side to side.

"They are out on a hike, due to be back in a few hours. I think they were going to have dinner in town." Gabby grabbed the pillow on her side and placed it in front of her, as if guarding her baby from the yelling she expected to occur.

"Spill it." Scarlett took a bite out of a cookie and waited. "I've seen you meandering about with the new guy in town. Is he staying?"

Gabby nodded. "Landon? Yes. Landon and I are now dating." She swallowed the rock that felt lodged in her throat.

"Darling, you didn't have to invite me over for cookies and tea just to tell me that. I saw the two of you in the park the other day. It was obvious you were moving on."

Gabby gripped the pillow tighter. Time to rip off the band aid. "There's something else, Scarlett." She took a deep breath and closed her eyes. "I'm pregnant with Parker's child."

Silence graced the air. The swing stopped swaying and a tiny gasp left Scarlett's mouth as the cookie clattered to the floor. "I already knew that, dear. I live in this town too, remember?" She clapped her hands together with glee. "This is such great news!"

Gabby opened her eyes and stared at the woman in disbelief. The squeal of excitement was not what she expected. "Scarlett, I'm not going to tell Parker."

That got her attention. "What?"

Gabby pulled the pillow closer. "I went to L.A. to see him, and he was with another woman. I couldn't tell him about the baby because at the time I wasn't sure it was his."

"But the baby is Parker's, right? You mean to tell me it could be Landon's? You sure didn't waste any time." Scarlett's voice had risen a few notches.

"I resent that," Gabby said, standing to face Scarlett. "I will not wait around for someone who has already moved on from me. Your son was selfish to decide for both of our futures without consulting me. I tried to be understanding, which is why I went to L.A. to begin with. Landon is kind, patient, and understanding. He's the one who convinced me to have this meeting with you. When and if Parker ever returns to Nano Springs, he can find out the news he's a father then. But I refuse to be that woman who chases after a man and gets him to take me back, all because I'm pregnant with his child."

Gabby threw the pillow onto the swing and marched towards the front door. "I think this meeting is over. You should go."

"Wait!" Scarlett called, the swing creaking as she stood. "I'm sorry. Please come back."

Gabby stopped and faced Scarlett but didn't go back to the sitting area. Scarlett dropped her outstretched hand and frowned. "I'm sorry. This was a lot of information to get in such a short time at my age. I will respect your decision to not tell my son about the baby. All I ask is, please don't shut me out."

"Scarlett, I loved your son. I still do in a small way. But I can't wait on him when he's disrespected our relationship. No matter what happens with Parker, or how my relationship with Landon turns out, you will always be this baby's grandmother." Gabby caressed her flat stomach as tears tickled the corners of her eyes.

"Thank you." Scarlett walked across the short distance of the porch and pulled Gabby into a hug. "My sweet girl. I'm so sorry for what my son has put you through. I'm here for you. This baby is going to be so loved."

Gabby nodded her head and wiped the tears from her eyes. "It will."

Scarlett led Gabby back to the porch swing and patted her hand. "Now, when do I get to meet this Landon?"

The sky had darkened, and the night insects were out playing their tune. Gabby rested her head on Scarlett's shoulder and sighed. Landon was staying at the apartment above Jen's Bookstore in town. He mentioned finding a cabin outside of town to buy and planned to meet with the relator by the end of the week. She wanted to let him settle in, and for the first time in her life, didn't feel the need to have someone by her side as often as before.

"The Labor Day celebration is next weekend. Landon promised to help set things up, so you'll likely see him then. He's busy looking for a place right now. The apartment wasn't meant to be long term," she said as the swing swayed back and forth.

"I look forward to meeting the man who made you smile again." They stay on swaying on the swing until the temperature dropped in the evening change. To be so close to the woman who mothered the man who broke her heart was bittersweet. She never believed parents were always responsible for their child's actions. It was a very gray area, in her opinion.

The idea of Scarlett meeting Landon when she herself barely knew him set a fire of anxiety in her chest ablaze. Gabby was far from caring what other people thought about her actions but, she refused to bring her baby into a world where those who loved her fought all the time. That was no environment for a child, or anyone for that matter. So why was she so worried about Scarlett meeting Landon? Would she break up the new relationship? Nah, Gabby agreed with Scarlett. Meeting Landon was the first time she'd smiled since Parker told her he was leaving Nano Springs.

Putting the worries behind her, they parted ways and Gabby began settling in for the evening. The next couple of weeks would be busy around the Inn and the town. She needed the rest if she wanted a successful event.

The amount of planning required for the town's Labor Day festivities let Gabby to lose herself; in schedules, budget meetings, and everything not related to her pregnancy. Each year the county selected a business to host the end of night event, which usually concluded with a spectacular fireworks show. Seeing as how the Inn sat perfectly on the lake, this year the risk for forest fires was extremely low.

Once the day arrived, Gabby stole a few moments alone in her office at the Inn. Morning sickness was subsiding, and she took that as a good sign. Still no word from Parker, and as more days passed, the less she expected him to even show his face. Their relationship was over. Accepting that fact took a little longer, but by the time she'd signed the last check for the event, she knew she'd be okay.

The townspeople helped pull everything together. Even if it was her business that hosted the event, everyone pitched in. Nano Springs centered on family and community, like a big church, or some other comparison where everyone was connected and respected the other. Landon dove in like a seasoned local and had the whole town accepting him with open arms. Gabby smiled as she closed her laptop and placed a hand over the cover.

The idea of dating again was daunting, and frankly, terrified her beyond words. A baby complicated things or could if she wasn't careful. She hated the idea of any tension or negativity surrounding the baby's birth, so Gabby did the only thing she could do. She took it one day at a time.

Landon differed from Parker, or any other man she'd encountered at the Inn. When he told her about his loss, instead of feeling sympathy and the need to fix things, as was her nature, she saw a man who was grieving in his own way. The painful void Parker created when he left still throbbed, but with every passing day, it lessened. Whether Landon was the cure, she could only speculate. But was that a bad thing? She deserved happiness, right?

Christina stepped into the office as Gabby reached for the cellphone to check her messages for the hundredth time that day.

"Parker may one day be my brother-in-law, but he doesn't deserve you, Gabby. Let him go."

Gabby tossed the phone down on the desk, where it landed with a thump. "I can't help but feel like there's something left undone," she said, laying her arm over her face. "Doesn't he deserve the right to know this is his kid?"

Gabby watched as Christina ran her hands down the length of her face. "For the love of God. If Parker walked in those doors right now, and said he wanted to be with you, would you want to after all of this?"

Christina didn't wait for a response as she rounded the desk and slammed her hand down firmly. "No. You wouldn't. Parker has made it clear he's moved on. You already said you didn't want him to come back just because you are having a baby," she sighed. She inhaled and lowered her voice. "Gabby, I'm so sorry that this relationship didn't work out. Most first loves don't. You know I wouldn't be saying this if I didn't love you. Give someone else a chance if you want to open your heart again. Even if Parker does return and wants a place in the baby's life, it doesn't mean he has to share your bed to do so."

The harsh truth of her friend's words vibrated around inside her brain. Instead of saying anything else, she wrapped her arms around Christina's shoulders. She was right. It was time to move forward. After Labor Day, she'd let herself enjoy this pregnancy and dream about the future that lay ahead. A future filled with promise, love, and a new sense of purpose. Gabby wiped away the tears that trickled from her eyes and whispered a thank you before shaking out her arms.

They spent a few moments together before leaving the office with a small list of to-do's before the firework finale. This year Gabby's parents were planning to pass the torch onto the younger generation, but not before one last row out to the barge that sat in the middle of the lake. The night sky darkened with sounds of laughter, sparklers, and joyful conversation. Gabby placed her hand on her lower belly. A small bump was beginning to form. One day she'd be holding a tiny human in her arms, and none of this will even matter.

The town event brought business to the entire area every year. The state papers picked up the story without hesitation. Finding good old- fashioned family fun these days was hard to come by. Nano Springs was the last small town in the area to even attempt to put on such a fanfare. Those who wanted to participate signed up months earlier for booths to showcase their business. A craft fair ran all weekend, rain or shine. Though the planning stages were intense and stressful, the actual day of was usually a laid-back affair.

Just before she took her place on the podium by the lake, Gabby stole a few minutes away in her suite. Standing before the floor- length mirror in a Navy-blue dress, she admired the subtle new curves her body had. Thankfully, the pregnancy wasn't so far along she had to replace the dress, though given another month and she wouldn't be so lucky. The brown trestles of hair escaping her tight bun gave off an angelic look that suited her well. *Girl, get over yourself,* she thought, reaching for her notecards lying on the bed. Just as she started for the door, she heard a gentle knock.

"Hey there," she said, opening the door. The man on the other side resembled Parker so strongly she had to catch the little gasp that threatened to escape. "I'm glad you came, Jacob."

"Yeah? I almost didn't, but Christina told me to get dressed and not be an ass. Can we talk?"

Parker's younger brother was as charming, as he was tough. The baby of the family, he was often spoiled at the hands of his mother. Despite that, he still had a compassionate side that made him fall head over heels for her best friend.

Gabby gestured to the couch in the sitting area and took a seat on one end. Jacob wore his usual outfit of blue jeans and a gray t-shirt that clung to his muscular frame. Jacob and Parker even shared the same crooked smile; one that said they knew they were in the wrong, but prayed you'd forgive them anyway.

Instead of joining her on the couch, he opted to lean against the door frame.

"Say what you need to say, Jacob. It's not like I haven't said the same thing to myself repeatedly." Gabby knew he would protect his brother, no matter how stupid Parker acted. It was a bond that connected them ever since their father walked out on the family when Jacob was six. Gabby didn't blame him, but she wouldn't have him judging her choices either.

"When I heard you'd started dating again, I was pissed. You've been like a sister to me all these years, even before you got involved with my brother. Then when Mom told me you and Parker were gonna be parents, I thought maybe you'd come to your senses."

"Ouch." Gabby crossed her legs and waited for him to finish.

"I'm still pissed, but not at you. I can't believe Parker would fu—screw up a good thing like this."

73

Gabby stood, embraced Jacob, and rested her head on his shoulder. "I'd never use your feelings against you Jacob, I understand the bond you have with Parker. But, that door swings both ways. You can't use my feelings against me either."

"I know, but what do you even know about this other guy? Lincoln or whatever his name is."

Gabby rolled her eyes. Jacob knew his name. "All I know is that he's here, and after everything I've told him...he's not running."

"I don't want you getting hurt," he said, exhaling.

"In less than 8 months, I'm going to be responsible for a tiny human. It's time for me to wear my own big girl panties, don't ya think?" She lay her hand on her stomach and gazed into his deep green eyes. "Now, let's put this behind us. People are going to wonder what happened to their host, so let's go."

Jacob and Gabby made their way onto the back deck and down the stairs towards the podium overlooking the lake. They were late to wish her parents a successful show, as the couple were arriving at the small barge as she stepped up to the microphone. Gabby nodded to Christina that things were okay and put a huge smile on her face. The stars overhead twinkled as the end-of-summer breeze carried the smells of grilled hot dogs, cotton candy, and popcorn through the wonderful community gathered to watch the show. This was where she was meant to be.

"Ladies and Gentlemen," she began, her voice booming loud over the speakers. "I want to thank everyone who made this day a success, and by everyone, I mean each of you. Each year we hold this event, no matter the host, it means so much to me and I am truly blessed to live among some of the most incredible neighbors, friends, and family. Now," she said, smiling and pointing towards the lake. "I'll shut up so we can get on with what you're really here for."

A loud boom vibrated against the trees around them as everyone on shore watched the first fireworks disperse from the platform. Her skin prickled and the hair on her arms rose as she watched the barge her parents were on explode in a giant ball of smoke and fire.

Chapter Eight

The search took three hours before the authorities found the charred bodies of Gabby's parents. Many of the men, gathered at the BBQ that evening, stripped themselves of their shoes and shirts to dive into the chilly waters. Instead of a rescue, they nearly got hypothermia, and now sat in the back of a couple of ambulances wrapped in fleece blankets. Sadly, there was no need for an ambulance for Gabby's parents.

Gabby stood stunned, unable to move from the spot at the edge of the podium. Her hands gripped the sides of the stand, crumbling the wood between her fingers. The flames rose high in the air, dissipating into smoke as the explosion made waves on the shore.

She felt the warmth of arms wrapping around her waist. Landon pulled her to his chest. "Sweetheart, let's go. We need to take you to the hospital. They need to check over you and the baby." The mention of the baby melted the shock from her brain and the tremors rocked her from head to toe. Before she went mute, she whispered where only he could hear. "Is this my life now? Constant pain with a little joy?"

The attention the Inn would get from this tragedy weighed heavily on Gabby's mind as the SUV bounced over the speed bump in the hospital parking lot. A glaring red sign that said *Emergency* bled into her vision as tears she'd been holding in fell easily from her eyes. How could one person go from being overwhelmingly happy one moment to utterly devastated the next? This wasn't life. It was a nightmare she wished she'd wake up from.

A slight flutter across her belly reminded her they'd never get to meet their grandchild. A nightmare. Gabby could feel her body shutting down. The will to stay awake or even alive began to lessen. She could feel her eyes get heavy and she thought about the life growing within her. She needed to fight through the grief. Gabby wasn't alone. As she climbed from the SUV, she saw half the town getting out of their cars; everyone who knew and loved Andy and Claire Lawson.

Landon stayed by her side during the exam, and she thanked the community for showing up and supporting her. Christina informed them she'd be in touch regarding services once they had time to figure all that out. At the car, she saw Jacob nod to Landon and mouth *thank you,* before leading Christina to his car beside them.

Chapter Nine

SEVEN MONTHS LATER

The mid-April afternoon smelled of roses in bloom and rain lurked behind dark gray clouds. It only took Landon eight months to learn how to sense when a good storm was heading their way. They'd had enough gloom in their lives since Gabby's parents passed away, and Landon fell over himself trying to keep her spirits up.

For the first month or two, Gabby showed up to work but was never fully present; she'd answer questions, complete her tasks, and greet the guests with a smile, but her eyes had lost their sparkle. The guests understood why she wasn't doing well. The owners were too polite to question her ability to run the inn, and expressed their condolences. Loss wasn't something that faded at a designated time. Grief didn't work on the same timetable for everyone.

The season ended without further excitement or causes for distress. Gabby locked herself in her room, only allowing Landon by her side. It elated that she felt comfortable enough with him, but he recognized what she was doing. Landon tried to explain to her that shutting out everyone that reminded her of her parents wasn't going to help, but he gave up before she tossed him out too.

Christina visited a few times. Landon could tell they were both trying, but there was a disconnect he hadn't been able to decipher. Maybe it had something to do with Christina's engagement to Jacob? Gabby didn't speak to him about any of it, but he was glad she let him comfort her.

The holidays brought the inevitable proposal between Jacob and Christina, and it was then that Gabby crumbled. Of course, she didn't show any of that emotion in front of her friend, but Landon spent many nights wiping tears from her eyes. She may not have explained why she was upset, but something was getting to her, and he hoped to figure it out sooner than later. He knew he shouldn't feel jealous of Parker, but he couldn't shake the feeling that Gabby's emotions were leading her back to thoughts of him. But who knew? Maybe he was wrong about that, too.

The bastard still hadn't even so much as sent a text since he left her eight and half months ago. Landon secretly hoped the guy wouldn't show his face again, but he knew at some point they'd run into each other. It was only a matter of time. He hoped soon Gabby would be ready to move forward, rather than backwards.

Landon turned his attention from the office window where he'd lost himself in thought and listened as the rumbling of thunder shook the thin glass. They'd made some repairs on the inn once the season ended, but there was still a long list of things to be fixed, the windows being one of them.

As he went over the paperwork of the last few months, he beamed with pride. He'd taken a keen understanding to stepping into the business management side of things while Gabby was grieving. He enjoyed knowing that when she returned, he'd be able to hand over things with order and no stress.

Gabby's mood swings reached new heights closer to her delivery date. One moment they'd be snuggling under the covers, having just finished a long day at the inn, the next she'd be crying over a commercial on the TV. The urge to retreat during the dark moments lay heavy at the center of their relationship. Flashbacks of how he left Jessica to deal with her mental health, changed his mind. Landon swore he'd never leave Gabby when she needed him.

If there were any lingering doubts about his feelings for Gabby, they'd disappeared the moment he felt the baby move. It was a month ago when she grabbed his hand at the dinner table and placed it on her growing stomach. The way her eyes lit up with joy, sucked him in and he realized he wanted more of that. He was in it, one hundred percent. She hadn't come out and said she loved him. Through the little gestures; the countless nights of sleeping in the same bed together, the way she looked at him from across the dinner table, and the electricity that passed through their hands when they touched, assured him they were okay.

Landon powered up his laptop that sat on the desk near the window. He hoped Brian would help him with an idea that brewed more and more every day. Brian didn't hesitate to let him off the hook with the business once he realized Gabby was pregnant. His friend gave him the usual talk of not getting in too deep, but all that changed when Gabby's parents died. He felt needed for the first time since Jessica's death, and he couldn't imagine leaving Gabby's side now.

"Brian?" he asked, looking at the screen as static blurred, the image fighting to come across. "There you are." Landon breathed a sigh of relief as his friend's oval face and brown eyes greeted him a moment later. His charcoal braids were tight against his head, and level with his shoulders.

"Everything okay, man?" Brian stood behind his desk chair,

not looking at the screen. Instead, he pushed his arms through a brown suit jacket and began buttoning the bottom buttons. "I have a meeting in ten, but you never use Skype anymore unless it's important. Gabby have the baby yet?"

Landon appreciated Brian being a phone call away when he needed him. Since the loss of his mother, and after Jessica died, Brian was the only person he could turn to on personal matters. The friend who refused to judge him whenever anyone else would call him weak for wearing his emotions on his shirt-sleeve.

"No. Still baking," he said, adjusting himself in the dark desk chair. He pulled his computer screen down to eliminate the glare from the window. The air conditioner kicked on and blew the bottom half of the *Def Leppard* poster away from the wall. He'd need to add another tack at the bottom. Ignoring the noise from the poster, Landon turned his attention back to his friend. He pulled down the sleeves of his work shirt and ran a hand through his blonde curls.

Brian checked his watch. "I'm listening."

When Landon told him what he wanted to do, he wasn't expecting the exasperated frustration to show across his friend's face. "I told you not to get wrapped up in this woman. Just friends, remember?"

Landon groaned. "What can I say? *This woman* stole my heart. Love doesn't have a time slot it clocks in at and appears when called. Sometimes things just happen and you fall. Man, I fell hard."

Brian stared blankly at the screen. It took Landon a moment to realize he was reading something on the other end. Instead of calling him out on not paying attention, Landon continued.

"Haven't you ever been in love, man? Maybe with someone you haven't mentioned?" Brian had done that before, though he hadn't been in love with the woman. He'd dated a woman for three months and ended it before Landon even had a clue.

Brian tore his eyes away from the document he was reading and smiled, a sarcastic gleam in his eyes. "I'm sitting here at my desk at two p.m., on a Friday afternoon, prepping for a meeting. So, no. I haven't found the love of my life yet. My job is the only lover I need right now."

"Right." Landon pushed away from the desk, then returned to the screen. "So, you're saying I shouldn't ask her?"

Brian stood and slung the briefcase strap over his shoulder. "It sounds like you have some decisions to make. Decisions I can't help you with, but I will say, guard your heart. Losing Jessica is still fresh. You don't want to end up back where you were before you left for Vermont." Before he hung up the call, Brian offered one last piece of advice. "If you love this girl, then tell her. Show her. I've got to run, but call me when you've figured things out. Good luck, man."

The screen went black. Landon slammed the laptop shut, feeling no better than when he initiated the call. He knew he should make a significant gesture, but not scare her off when she's the most vulnerable. He wanted Gabby to see that Parker was her past and Landon was her future.

He stepped to the window and pulled the curtains even further back to let the light in. He'd always loved natural light over any other. Recognizing the woman carrying a large box, Landon rushed down to help Gabby's best friend with the package. As he took the steps two at a time, an idea began to form in his mind.

"Hey! Let me help you with that," he offered, reaching for the box in Christina's hand a minute later. "Listen, I have an idea for a special evening for Gabby, but as someone who's known her longer, I wanted to run it by you first."

"Um, sure," Christina said, matching his step into the lodge. "I'm all ears. Where is Gabby, anyway?"

Landon waved off her question as he set the box down inside the door. "She's stepped out. Shouldn't be much longer."

"Okay then, I have a few minutes. What's your idea?"

As he led her to a couch in the guest area, a prickle of excitement ran up the nape of his neck.

THAT EVENING, Landon stood on the steps of the Inn, inhaling the summer air. The crickets had come out, and played their nightly tune. A sound Landon was beginning to enjoy the longer he lived in Nano Springs.

A light click of the door behind him interrupted the moment, as he turned and smiled at Gabby. Her swollen belly clung to the deep purple sleeveless dress she wore for their date night. Her hair was pinned to one side with a sparkling clip, and the tendrils lay over her shoulders.

"Can you please tell me where we're going?" she asked, placing a hand against her lower back.

"You'll just have to wait and see. It's a surprise," he said, playfully.

Christina didn't support his plan for the evening, but thankfully, his decision to move forward didn't depend on anyone else's opinion. He'd only asked to see if Christina thought Gabby would run for the hills. Landon knew, especially as he watched Gabby pull her seatbelt across her body, that he was doing the right thing. They'd come so far in their relationship in the last seven months. He was confident the night would turn out the way he wanted. Christina's concern for Gabby being in a fragile state did try to work its way into his mind. Pushing the thought aside, he shifted the car into gear and slowly backed out of the parking lot.

The ring box in his back pocket was in the worst position, but there was nowhere else to put it, except in the bags he'd packed for them both. He didn't want Gabby accidentally finding it later before he could present the beautiful diamond ring to her himself. Landon readjusted himself and ignored the pain until they could get to where they were going.

Gabby was the fresh air he never knew he needed until their first meeting. There were still days that he thought of Jessica and their unborn baby, but Jessica made the choice to leave him. He'd always miss her and the good times they had together, but grieving forever didn't sit well with him. Not when he was still young enough to move on and still live a happy life. *Was that selfish?* Gabby gave him that happiness, and after tonight, he hoped she'd give him forever.

Landon ran his sweaty palms over his black dress slacks before grabbing hold of Gabby's hand. He placed their hands on the middle console of the SUV and gave it a squeeze. "Tonight is meant to be fun, okay? Trust me?"

Gabby brought their hands to her mouth and pressed her lips to his before responding. "I do. I trust you, Landon." She didn't take her eyes from him, and he didn't want to stop looking at her. But he couldn't gaze into her eyes within the darkness of the car, and besides, someone needed to drive the car.

They made small talk on their way out of town. Over the next half hour, he fielded her playfully childish questions of, "Are we there yet?" and "Where are we going?" Before they reached their turn, Landon pulled the wheel of the SUV over to the side of the road. "We're almost there," he said, reaching into the backseat. He grabbed the soft blindfold he'd placed there earlier that evening. With a seductive smile, that could be seen from the dash lights, he asked, "how much do you trust me?"

"I'll admit," she said, grabbing the blindfold with her thumb and index finger, "I'm a little turned on."

He laughed and steered the car back onto the road. "Even better than I thought. Now when I say, slip that on, okay?"

They drove in silence for another ten minutes before he gave her a gentle nudge. "Okay, babe. Here we are." The dirt road ahead showed no signs of what the endgame was, and Landon could feel his excitement grow. He knew from their time together, she enjoyed surprises that didn't involve being hurt, and she loved the simple things in life.

He watched as Gabby slipped the blindfold over her eyes. A small smile formed on her lips as she made a seductive show of tying it behind her head.

"Done."

His heart skipped a beat when he caught the hint of flirting in her voice. *Could this work?*

Landon pressed the gas and took them up a winding road covered in darkness. They stayed like this for a few minutes before coming through a clearing littered with white Christmas lights strung along the trees. The place looked even better in the evening. To the right, he saw the town of Nano Springs lit up like a storybook setting. The lake glistened in the moonlight down below.

The lights on the tall, three-story house set off a spectacular ambiance that set the tone for the entire evening. He almost told Gabby to remove the blindfold, but it wasn't time yet. Landon knew it was a risk to bring her to a bed- and- breakfast, seeing as she lived and worked at a version of one. This place was different, more private. As he opened the door, the wind blew the trees around him, their leaves sending up a wave of applause. Okay, maybe he was patting himself on the back too early.

"Landon?" Gabby asked, still sitting in the passenger seat. "Did you bring me all this way to abandon me in the car? Cause if so, this isn't what I'd call a date night," she said, a light hesitation in her voice.

He hadn't meant to worry her, and he rushed to her side and helped her from the car before it got out of hand. "Stand right there. I need to get some things from the car. I was admiring the view." A moment later, he had both bags in one hand, and his other guided Gabby towards the large white staircase.

"We must be really far up in the mountain," she noted. "I haven't heard the crickets this loud in ages. The air smells fresh too, woodsier."

Instead of answering for fear he'd give the secret away, Landon opened the screen door and gave a hard knock. Minutes later, a short, gray-haired woman greeted them with a friendly smile. She ushered them inside and handed Landon a key on a feathered keychain. They'd taken care of the arrangement earlier in the day, so all that was left was to go to the room.

"Okay, I'm getting a little nervous here," Gabby said, reaching for the blindfold.

"Wait! I promise, just a few more steps and you can take it off."

Landon nodded his thanks to the innkeeper and made his way up the wooden steps that sat in the center of the entryway. They'd have time to explore the rest of the place in the morning, but for now, he had a view he didn't want Gabby to miss. In their room, he placed the suitcases down by the door and guided her further inside towards the balcony.

Once they were standing in front of the open sliding glass doors, he removed the blindfold and watched her entire face light up. Her reaction made his heart swell bigger than it ever had before.

When he'd stopped by earlier that day, he'd strung up a winding line of white lights along the railing. The effect was better than he imagined. An ambiance set the ultimate romantic mood. The crickets did their job and he admitted, they were louder the higher they got into the mountains.

From the balcony, they could see the entire town down below as well as the lake. Of course, the lake wasn't much of a happy place these days. Gabby admitted she was trying to find a way to enjoy it, regardless of the bad memories it held. The town though, the view during the holidays had to be epic. This was now their place, an escape from work and home. Now that they were there, the ring felt heavier than ever in his pocket. He'd wanted to wait until morning, while they were eating breakfast in bed, but he wasn't sure he could wait another minute.

After a moment of silence between the two of them, Gabby turned and wrapped her arms around Landon's waist. She gazed at him with those adoring eyes and smiled. "In all my years growing up in this town, I never knew this place existed. How did you find it?"

He kissed her forehead before saying, "The innkeeper, Ms. Otis, recently lost her husband and move here to open their dream business. A home where they could welcome people of all walks of life, and spend time together, even if just briefly. When I found the website online, we emailed back and forth where she told me the story and how it was their dream come true."

"Hmm, what a lovely story."

There were two white rocking chairs on the balcony, and he gestured towards one as he explained how he stumbled onto the bed and breakfast. He knew he wanted to do something special for her before the baby came. Landon didn't have much experience with babies, but he knew once they arrived, they became the number one thing to most moms. Gabby would need the rest and relaxation before the little one's arrival. They hadn't found out the sex, and he'd agreed when Gabby told him she wanted it to be a surprise.

Once she looked comfortable in the chair, he knelt in front

of her and took her hands in his. It was as if the crickets knew he had something important to say as they all fell silent.

"I know we haven't spoken much more about what brought me out here. I've made my peace with Jessica's decision, and I'm ready to move forward with my life," he said, enjoying the way the lights hit her face. She was glowing.

"Are you leaving?" she said, pulling her hands away.

He refused to let go of her hands. "No! Not at all, unless you ask me to go, I'll be here. Let me finish?" Landon offered a smile before continuing. "I know we don't know each other as well as some couples. I know you're having a baby that's not mine. I know we may get looks in town if this goes the way I hope. But, Gabby, none of that matters. I want to spend the rest of my life getting to know the beauty that is inside you. I want to spend the rest of my life helping you take care of and love that little one coming into our lives soon. I want to spend the rest of my life watching the gossips in town talk about how amazing we are together, and how despite everything, we took our second chances and made dreams come true out of them. Gabby, will you marry me?"

Chapter Ten

The air around them stilled as she stared at the blue box with white velvet, a one caret diamond ring sitting in the center. White lights on the railing bounced off the ring, making it glow beautifully in Landon's palm. Many thoughts raced through her mind; Landon wanted to be with her despite the baby not being his. He'd never left her side the last seven months, unless she told him she needed a few moments alone. She enjoyed his company and it wasn't until that moment that she realized how much she'd grown to love him. The beautiful man was everything she wanted in a committed relationship. It was clear he loved her too. The baby, who wasn't even born yet, seemed to hold his heart as well.

Gabby felt the first tear trickle down her cheek as she slowly held out her left hand. Seven months ago, she'd said goodbye to Parker. Giving herself the only closure she'd likely get at this point. It was time to open her heart to someone else, and trust that she wasn't destined to be alone at twenty-six. Landon not only broke down the barrier around her heart, but he also did it in such a loving way. He showed her what commitment really look liked. Before, she'd been afraid of moving forward. It was time to stop being afraid.

"Yes," she whispered. One hand rested on her heart as he slid the ring perfectly onto her finger. Even with swollen fingers, the ring fit like it was made for her. Once the ring was in place, she struggled to her feet. "I love you, Landon. Thank you for reminding me what love really looks like and for being patient with me as I figured things out on my own." She glanced down at her belly between them. "First things first," she said, laughing.

"Of course," Landon agreed.

The crickets picked up their favorite tune again as Landon took Gabby in his arms. She titled her head slightly to meet his kiss with her lips as he swayed them gently back and forth. He tasted like heaven; sweet wine and sunkisses. Gabby couldn't wait to be drunk on his love every day. She still thought of Parker, but now she only wished he were as happy as she was. It was clear to her, they weren't meant to be together, and it took the separation to make her see the bigger picture.

Gabby placed her hands against his chest, stopping the moment. She slipped one hand in his and led him back into the bedroom. The lights were still off as the ones from the balcony gave plenty. She liked it that way. "Leave the door open. It's such a beautiful night."

The dress was beginning to become uncomfortable as her stomach tightened and she was dying to get out of it anyway. She sat on the edge of the bed and awkwardly removed her flip flops. They were the only comfortable shoes she owned at this time in her pregnancy. Thankfully, they didn't take a lot of effort. Sadly, her dress was another story. It clung to her swollen frame as she stood up and looked helplessly at Landon who was leaning against the door frame.

"Help, please?" she asked, turning to face the bed, offering him her back.

The warmth of his fingers near the nape of her neck sent chills down her spine.

Being pregnant made her hesitant, especially this far along in her pregnancy, but the growing desire pushed that away as fast as the thought appeared. It would be a while before she was able to be intimate once the baby came. She missed the touch of a man and the pleasure that came with a touch.

"Are you sure?" Landon whispered as his lips trailed the line of her neck. "I had no expectations of tonight, love. Only the hope that you'd accept the ring and make me the happiest man alive. Anything else is just a bonus," he said, unclipping the back of her dress. She felt him hesitate and she reached up and pulled the straps down over her shoulders.

"I've never been sure of anything else," she said, turning to face him as her dress dropped to the soft carpet around her feet. Gabby placed both hands over the small stubble that had formed on his face over the last few weeks. She loved the softness now that it had grown from the prickly texture. She pulled his face to hers and entrapped his lips in her own, savoring the desire stirring throughout her body.

Later, once they'd exhausted themselves, they found soft plush bathrobes in the closet. Wrapping themselves in the fabric, they lay side by side, his hand resting on her belly. She felt his warm breath on her neck as he gave a light kiss before she succumbed to a sweet slumber.

A mere hour passed of peaceful sleep when suddenly her body folded over, as she grunted and cried out in excruciating pain. It felt as if the baby was trying to rip itself from her body.

"Gabby? Babe? What's wrong?" Landon asked, leaning over her with concern in his eyes. She couldn't talk, the pain was too great as she sat forward and felt between her legs. When she lifted her hand, the clear, warm liquid covered her palm.

Labor. Gabby was in labor.

. . .

AN INCESSANT ALARM shrilled near Gabby's head. She licked her cracked lips and coerced her eyes open. Through the slits she saw Landon sleeping in a chair next to her bed. His head rested on his palm, threatening to drop at any moment. The strain of the day was clear by the shade of purple under his eyes.

Her mind buzzed as she searched the room for a clock, trying to remember the events that unfolded once she realized her water broke. Poor Ms. Otis would need a visit once she got out of the hospital, and an apology for destroying her flowered bedding. It felt like days had passed, as she remembered the ambulance ride to the hospital. All she could remember was how scary everything was; the paramedics ripping the robe from her body, jamming in an IV line into her arm, and the oxygen mask drowning out the sirens shrilling from outside.

The clock on the wall read ten-thirty and by the darkness from the single window across from the bed, Gabby realized she'd been out for forty-five minutes. Despite the comfort of prayer, she couldn't control her breathing and that was when she blacked out.

What a way to spend their engagement night. Apparently, sex had done more than she expected. She blushed as she thought back to their time together. Gabby looked over at Landon and winced when she realized he was staring at her with a small smile on his face.

"Hey beautiful. You look happier," he said, standing to stand next to the bed.

"Yeah, just thinking about earlier." She brushed the thought away with a swipe of her hand in the air. The baby blue blanket draped over her legs made her skin itch. She tugged it up, careful not to slap herself in the face. A chill lingered in the air, and she wasn't sure if it was because the hospitals insisted on keeping the rooms freezer cold or fear about going into labor a month early. She placed her arms on either side of her and turned her attention to Landon. "What happened?"

The sound of his chair scraping across the gray speckled tile grated in her ears. He moved closer and sat down before he answered, his voice a soft hum of comfort. "You gave me quite the scare. The paramedics said you had some sort of a panic attack on the way here."

Gabby nodded, rubbing her stomach with the palm of her right hand. It made sense. She'd been prone to panic attacks since she was younger. The doctors didn't really know why they struck during some stressful situations and not others, but it was something she dealt with her entire life. Peeking from under her bangs, she asked the question she was most afraid to be answered. "The baby?"

Landon smiled and stood to pull down the metal bed rail. He sat on the edge of the bed and took her hand. "She's perfectly okay. I got to see her on the ultrasound they did when you first came in, and she's still moving and looks great."

"I'm having a girl?" she asked, clasping her hands together. The blood pressure cuff interrupted her celebration for a moment, jolting her body before she relaxed as it gave her upper arm a squeeze. Images of a perfect baby girl flashed across her vision; one with her on Gabby's chest, in Landon's arms as he looked out over the lake from the back patio, a happy family picture for sure. For a moment, Parker's face butted in, but she quickly shut it out. She was grateful for their years together, and of course without him she wouldn't be a mom soon, but he had his chance. For all she knew, he was still in L.A., living his life and not even thinking about her.

Taking a deep breath, she pressed Landon's palm to her lips and whispered, "We're having a girl!" An idea began to form in her mind and as she stared at the ring still sitting snug on her finger. "How would you feel about putting your name on the birth certificate?" she asked. Gabby watched Landon's face to see his initial reaction, thinking he'd get scared and disagree. It wasn't common, or maybe it was, she didn't know. If they were going to make this official, then they needed to go all the way. It felt right, that's all that mattered to Gabby.

"You want to name me as the father?" he asked, his face blank but his eyes straining a bit at the corners. "Is that even allowed? I don't know how legal stuff like that goes, but could we run into problems down the road?"

"Listen," she said, dropping his hand. "If this scares you too much, you don't have to do anything you don't want to do. Parker may eventually come back into the picture, but rest assured, he'll never take my heart from you. I don't know the state rules about these things either. It's not like it was something I set out to do from the beginning," she said, shifting her body sideways a smidge.

Landon quickly grabbed her hand back into his. "No, I'm not saying I don't want to do this. I asked you to be my wife, Gabby. As far as I'm concerned, we're already heading towards a lifetime. This baby has already gotten the other half of my whole heart. I just want you to be sure."

Before they could continue the conversation, Dr. Matthis walked into the room with such dramatic flair Gabby lost all train of thought. He smiled at them both before checking the screen that showed the baby's heartbeat. "Another contraction, huh?" he asked, running his index finger along the paper coming from the machine. "It looks like little Miss is a strong one." He sat on the stool at the foot of the bed and wheeled himself to the opposite side of the bed from Landon. Dr. Matthis pulled out his stethoscope from his lab coat pocket and began his exam. Gabby was so happy he'd be delivering the baby. Being so far away from the Inn, in the next town over, she was worried they'd end up at the county hospital and not Nano Springs Memorial. When prompted she took in a deep breath and let it out, repeating it three more times. A groan escaped her lips, the site of the poorly placed IV began to throb, causing her to wince.

"Your arm could be sore for a few days. I'm sorry about County EMT's, you know they don't know jack about inserting IVs or working the needle." Doctor Matthis always had an opinion about anyone who worked anywhere that wasn't Nano Springs. He took pride in his work, and it was one of the reasons Gabby liked the man. It didn't hurt that he'd been the same doctor to deliver her when she first came into the world.

"Do you think I'll have the baby today?" she asked, hopefully. As much as she knew babies needed to bake as long as possible, she was more than ready to meet her little girl.

"Because your water already broke, and baby girl is measuring well, I think we can deliver today. No reason to wait." He'd hardly gotten the last word out before he reached for her left hand and held it up to the light.

"I see even more congratulations are in order?" he asked, eyes Landon before smiling down at Gabby. "I'm so happy to see you happy, Gabs. After everything you've been through this year, you deserve it."

"Thank you, Doctor," she said, glancing lovingly at Landon.

Doctor Matthis patted her hand and released it. "Let Nurse Ashley know if you need anything. Only ice chips from here on out and we should be able to get started shortly."

After a few more questions, Gabby closed her eyes and drifted into a light sleep as the delivery team prepared for her daughter's birth. She shifted in the bed and wrestled with her nightmares. Losing Parker would always have a small effect on her, especially looking at his child every day. She fought to push the pain away and thought of the happiness she had with

Landon. She'd finally get the family she wanted; the job she desired, and the life she deserved.

"Babe?" Landon asked, kissing her on her cheek. "I think they are ready."

Now that he'd mentioned it, the contractions did feel stronger. She opened her eyes and gripped the railing, gritting her teeth as she blew out hard and moaned.

"Oh boy," Landon said. He clamped his mouth shut when she cut her eyes at him.

Once the contraction passed, she leaned back against the limp pillow and motioned for the nurse in between her heavy breathing.

"What can I get you, hon?" Nurse Ashley was a beautiful woman. Her blonde hair was braided in a French braid down her back. She had wide brown eyes and a smile any dentist would love.

"Can I get a better pillow?" she asked.

"Of course, I'll be right back."

When Ashley was gone, Gabby pulled Landon to her, gripping the front of his shirt in the process. Thankfully, he'd changed from the robe they'd went to bed in and now he wore a plain white T-shirt that clung to his frame. His blue jeans hung perfectly at his slender waist. She loved the man and needed to hear him say he's all in.

"Is that a yes on the birth certificate?"

"Yes, Gabby. Forever and Always, yes." He planted a kiss on her forehead as she released his shirt. Another contraction gripped her, and she knew it was time to meet her baby girl. Their baby girl.

The nurse returned to the room with a pillow that was far more comfortable than the one before. As she thanked the her, a strong contraction ripped through her. Gabby saw spots and leaned forward with tears forming in her eyes. Labor hurt like a bitch.

An orderly came in to help the nurse prep the bed; pulling off the bottom and setting up the stirrups. Gabby glanced at Landon, who'd begun to sweat and pace in the small square where he stood. They were ready; to close the current chapter and begin a brand new one. As another contraction gripped her from the inside, she closed her eyes and thought about how childbirth would change her life.

Chapter Eleven

L andon sat on the shower chair in the delivery room bathroom, a pair of hospital scrubs waited for him on the counter. In a matter of minutes, he'd be a father and there was no turning back. He wanted Gabby and the baby in his life more than anything, but now that the time had come, he had to admit he was panicking a little. What would Parker's family think about him swooping in and changing everything? Should he even care?

"Mr. Marshall?" A gentle knock jolted him up and he cracked the door open.

"Yes?"

"We wanted to let you know that Ms. Lawson was asking for you. Also, here's the paperwork you need to sign." The nurse, a male this time, passed a stapled packet through the crack with a pen attached.

"Okay, I'll take care of these and please tell Gabby I'll be out soon."

Once the door closed again he placed the papers on the counter and stared at his reflection in the mirror. His sandy blonde hair was turning a lighter shade of brown, and his eyes were bright with excitement. He'd put on a few pounds, but he not enough that his clothes didn't fit. There were now lines near his eyes, but the past eight months brought on new stresses that changed him.

Landon turned his attention to the paperwork. There was a blue tab off to the side where he needed to sign. A moment of truth. Was he ready to put his name on the birth certificate? Without hesitation, he signed his name. Committing to a lifetime of protection, love, and unity to a little girl who already stole his heart from the womb. *Ready or not,* he thought as he capped the pen and reached for the scrubs.

THE LIGHTS WERE DIMMED, and the blinds were closed over the darkened window in the corner. Landon put his bag on the chair near the door and stood at the head of Gabby's bed. Dr. Matthis hadn't arrived, but the delivery team seemed ready and in place. He noticed another nurse double checking supplies in what could only be described as a baby warmer. Gabby was situated in a seated position, the air escaping between her lips in quick short breaths.

"Nice of you to show up," she said, a low grunt rumbling from her chest.

"I'm so sorry babe," he said, rubbing his hand along her back.

"Please don't touch me right now, I'm sorry, but you're breaking my focus."

He tried not to be offended. In all the pregnancy books he devoured over the last several months, he expected some sort of displaced frustration. As he contemplated what words to say that wouldn't have her snapping at him, Dr. Matthis breezed into the room, stretching on a pair of latex gloves.

"Looks like you're ready to have a baby, Ms. Lawson."

For the next forty-five minutes, Gabby gripped his hand and gave push after push. Landon tried dabbing a wet cloth on her forehead, but he felt utterly helpless as her face became redder and redder. "You have to breathe, babe," he said, praying she'd have the baby soon. Her restraint frightened him. This was not how the pregnancy books explained a mother giving birth. Landon failed to see the beauty in pushing with not progress.

"One more big push," Dr. Matthis said, encouraging Gabby from under the blue cloth that lay over her lap.

Landon stood frozen as Gabby squeezed his hand so hard he could almost hear the bones break. She was a superwoman. As he gazed upon her face, he heard the most beautiful sound, the baby's cry. Strong and healthy and oh so gorgeous, Landon could barely see through his tears.

The doctor held the baby above the blue cloth and then placed her on Gabby's stomach. Landon took one lingering look at the baby; pale peach skin with dark black hair, and immediately he knew he'd never love anything more than her. As Landon tore his eyes from the baby to congratulate Gabby— he noticed Gabby's eyes roll back in her head.

He lowered the rail like he'd seen the nurses do earlier and leaned over Gabby's body. "Don't do this to me, sweetheart," he said, patting her cheeks, fighting not to shake her awake.

A nurse brushed him aside and began checking Gabby's airway. Another nurse reached for a needle in the cart behind him as Nurse Ashley ushered him into a nearby waiting room. Before he could ask her what happened, she bolted back through the doors, leaving him shivering in the room alone.

Chapter Twelve

THE TICK of the minute hand on the clock in the hallway did little to comfort Landon's fear about Gabby. Seconds ticked by as if nothing mattered; not his heart breaking or the fact it'd been a half hour with no word on Gabby's condition.

Sure, the doors to the delivery room opened once, but he couldn't see anything behind the curtain. A nurse rushed out only to return seconds later with IV bags filled with blood.

Landon pushed himself off the wall where he'd been leaning, the weight of his worry made holding himself up rather difficult. He paced, anxious for news but his faith wavered every time the minute hand moved another line. After all they'd been through, the things they'd overcome together; abandonment, pain, heartache, would it really all end here?

The baby was rushed to the nursery one floor up, but Landon trusted the staff to care for his daughter. He needed to be there, outside the room, close to Gabby. He couldn't lose her. This wasn't how their chapter was supposed to close.

"Landon?" Christina and Jacob walked through the brown double doors at the end of the hall. He'd forgotten the phone call he made before Gabby had the baby, inviting the pair to the hospital. Gabby's hospital bag was left at the Inn since he didn't think she would be having the baby for another month. Christina offered to grab it on their way.

"Did Gabby have the baby?" she asked, her bright eyes wide with excitement. "What are you doing out here?"

After a moment he peered up at Christina's worried face. The light had gone from her eyes as she reached for Jacob's hand. *Must be nice to have someone to comfort you when you're scared out of your mind,* he thought. "Gabby had a complication after the delivery," he said, watching a patient being wheeled down the hall on a gurney. Once the hall was empty again, Landon stood up and leaned his head back against the wall. "The baby is fine." Landon's heart skipped a beat as he remembered the strong cry of Gabby's baby. His daughter. "Guy's, she's beautiful."

Jacob and Christina stood identically with their arms folded across their bodies. Their jeans were crisp and clean as if they'd just come off the rack. Matching blue and red T-shirts clung to their slender frames. He wondered why he noticed their clothes at a time like this. Maybe because it meant not focusing on the inevitable.

His voice lost its calm as frustration seeped in once more. "Gabby lost consciousness a few minutes after the birth, she hardly even got to hold the baby. One minute my heart is soaring with happiness at how strong the baby sounded despite being premature, to watching Gabby's grip loosen and her head fall to the side," he said, fresh tears prickling at the corner of his eyes. "Next thing I know they push me out here like a dog who doesn't know his place."

Landon didn't mind the fact Christina tried to comfort him, but it wasn't her arms he wanted around him. It was killing him not to be in the room with Gabby. Landon couldn't say that they'd been romantic and madly in love. It was still new despite everything feeling at warp speed right then. If he was honest with himself, their relationship had been more of a need for survival. Being abandoned, hurt, and they'd both spent hours talking about the pain of not being enough for someone. For once in their lives, they felt like they were finally enough. Gabby obviously felt the same way, not only did she tell him, but showed him by putting his name on the birth certificate.

Did she know? Was she aware she could die in childbirth? He hoped not. Landon loved the idea of being the baby's father. This was his second chance. But losing Gabby was not how he wanted things to go. There was so much more to their story.

Landon had to get in there.

Pushing Christina's arms away from him, he stole one last glance at Jacob and tried to push open the delivery room doors. Landon wiped my eyes; he didn't want Gabby to see him crying. He needed to be strong for her. As soon as his hand gripped the door handle, Landon felt a pair of strong hands pull him backwards. Jacob's voice was in his ear, and the more he fought against him, the tighter Jacob's embrace became.

"You won't be of any help to her right now if you walk through those doors, Landon," Jacob said, his teeth clenched, though Landon sensed no anger in his voice. "You'll only distract them from caring for Gabby. "A change of scenery will do you good."

"I'm not leaving the hospital," Landon said, shrugging from Jacob's embrace. "I won't leave without her."

"Okay, we don't have to leave the hospital. Have you seen the baby yet?" Christina placed her hand on Landon's arm. "Let's go to the nursery and see her."

He hesitated as he turned towards the door again. Jacob clapped him on the shoulder, causing him to jump. "Only for a moment, then I need to come back here. I never want her to feel like I abandoned her."

"They'll know where to find you, man. I'm sure they'll page you if anything else happens." Jacob gripped Landon by the shoulders and steered him down the hall.

Five minutes. He'll go make sure their baby was okay, and then he'd return to be as close to Gabby as the hospital staff would allow. Everything was supposed to be better for them. They'd found each other. They were happy. Landon walked with his head down, his thoughts racing wildly. He should know better by now, nothing in life was ever as easy as it should be.

THE SLANTED LINES of the nursery window blurred in his vision. The moisture in his eyes made it difficult to see the baby in her plastic bassinet. Landon hated calling her "the baby" but he didn't want to name her without Gabby. Up until he proposed, he'd left that decision to her.

Would he have to name the baby on his own? It's not as if he couldn't but doing so would mean losing Gabby and that wasn't something he was ready for. He needed to get back to her and he cursed himself for allowing Jacob and Christina to take him away from the delivery area. "I'm going back upstairs," he said, tapping lightly on the glass window.

Landon glanced into the nursery and watched a nurse offer the baby a pacifier to calm her. Too bad nothing could soothe the worry etched into his heart. When the pacifier wouldn't work, the nurse picked the baby up and nuzzled her against her chest. He knew he should go in and hold the baby, the nurse had motioned him in earlier, but he hadn't wanted to lay his concern on the infants shoulders. Babies could sense things most adults couldn't; just another thing he read in the countless baby books he'd bought when he found out Gabby was pregnant.

"We just got here. Maybe you should go in and hold her?" Christina raised her hand and gently tapped the glass, motioning to the nurse that Landon wanted to go inside the room. While he waited for the nurse to open the door, he peered down the well-lit hallway, the florescent lights lit up the pale pink bunnies hung along the equally pale blue wall.

He said a silent prayer that'd he'd be able to comfort her without reflecting his negative energy onto her as he stepped through the door. A few moments later, after putting the pink paper scrubs on over his clothes, he rocked in the light brown rocking chair near the bassinet. The baby lay on his chest, as he pondered Parker's earlier phone call. It wasn't a shock that Parker would reach out at some point, but Landon wouldn't lie to himself that it didn't rattle him.

Gabby accepted his proposal. They were planning a life together, but would that still hold true if she knew Parker wanted back into her life? That right there was why he hadn't said anything. Even if Gabby wouldn't have said, "yes," he still didn't think Parker deserved her. The guy had his chance and screwed that up. Landon wouldn't be possessive over the baby or Gabby for that matter, but Gabby needed to be able to move forward. She'd told him months ago that she got her closure, slowly, as the months of silence drug on. If he didn't think she was ready to move on, he'd never had proposed to begin with.

The baby began to fuss and squirm, and he realized he'd stopped rocking. As he picked up the rhythm again, he inhaled the scent of baby shampoo. A nurse named Emberly, offered a burp cloth over his shoulder. He smiled politely and rub the baby's back before whispering, "Baby girl, I promise you when your mama makes it through this, we'll take you home and make you the center of our world. You'll never have to worry about anything." His voice caught once and he closed his eyes, finally feeling himself relax a little bit. He needed to have more faith if they had a chance of getting past this. Gabby just had to be okay.

Landon stayed in the nursery for a total of twenty-five minutes before he couldn't take the suspense anymore. It had been more than an hour since they'd kicked him out of the delivery room, he needed answers. "I'll be back soon, Princess. I need to go check on your Mama." He kissed the baby on her soft black hair and returned her to the awaiting nurse.

"I'll take real good care of her Mr. Marshall," Emberly said, taking the baby from his arms. "She's a real sweetheart already."

"Thank you." He leaned in to kiss the baby once more before stepping out the door, pulling it closed behind him with a click.

Christina and Jacob sat huddled together on the floor under the nursery windows. They stood when he appeared and offered small smiles. "You're really good with her," Christina said, embracing him in a hug. When she stepped back he noticed her frown. "Jacob and I were talking, and we were wondering what was going to happen with you and Gabby now that the baby is here?"

They couldn't be serious. Landon took a step back, his hands running nervously through his hair. He was tired, frustrated, and worried. He couldn't believe Christina would ask him that. Not after they still didn't know what was going on with Gabby.

"What's going to happen is, I'm going upstairs and will find a doctor or nurse and demand they tell me something about my *fiancée*", he said, emphasizing fiancée. "Then, I'm going to wait as close to her room as possible until I can bring her and the baby home with me."

If things weren't so tense, he would have laughed and told Jacob to pick his chin up off the floor. Landon bet the guy didn't expect the news that Gabby had really moved on. But, in that moment, he didn't care. Without another word to either of them, Landon turned and marched down the hallway towards the elevator.

ONCE HE ARRIVED on the delivery floor, he strode up to the nurse's station and asked for Dr. Matthis. "Sir, Dr. Matthis is unavailable at this time. If you have a seat in the waiting area, I'll send him out as soon as he's available," said a young nurse.

The phone in her hand seemed more important than her job, as she tapped her fingers across the screen. Landon was done waiting for answers. He clinched his fist and brought it down hard on the counter in front of him. "It's been over an hour since my fiancée had our daughter and passed out. I need to know how she's doing, and I won't sit down until I get some fucking answers."

He didn't mean to yell, it wasn't who he was; a bully, someone who demanded things from other people. But he couldn't shake the coldness that began to creep up his spine the longer he was away from Gabby. The doubt alone was eating him up. What if she woke up and decided she wasn't ready to move on? He wouldn't be able to handle it if this traumatic event caused her to rethink everything from the past nine months. Landon didn't think he could take another loss. Even playing out the different scenarios in his mind now seemed selfish.

His hair probably looked like something you'd see on a psych patient, and his clothes were beginning to suffocate him. Was he having a panic attack?

"Landon, it's okay." Christina's voice behind him made him jump. "If they had any news for you, they'd be out here. You need to remain calm, or they'll kick you out of the hospital." She smiled at the nurse and tried to get him to go to the waiting room.

"No!" Christina jumped at the sound of his voice, so he lowered it a notch. "I'm sorry, but I can't go sit in a waiting room. You go. I'll wait right here." He walked over to the delivery room door and leaned against the wall. They couldn't make him move; he wouldn't let them.

He noticed Jacob wasn't with her anymore and figured small talk was better than the silence. The only sounds he heard were the overhead announcements paging random doctors he didn't know, and the occasional cart being wheeled down the hallway, the wheels squeaking and adding to his growing headache.

"Where's Jacob?"

Christina leaned against the wall next to him. "I sent him home. Scarlett is flying in tonight and I told him he needed to be there to greet her when she arrived and fill her in."

Oh right, the grandmother. How was all this going to work?

This weird family dynamic. He wouldn't contest to Parker's mother being in their lives, it's not as if she did anything wrong, but how would she react to the news of their engagement? Had Parker called her?

So many questions rumbled through his brain. The whirl-wind their lives had taken nearly left him breathless. He could do this though. Gabby meant the world to him, and the baby, *damn we need to name her,* had already stolen his heart. There was no turning back now.

"I can't lose her, Christina. I know you didn't think proposing was a good idea when we spoke last, but we're both ready for this commitment." He swiped the exhaustion from his eyes and stared at the tiled floor.

"I know. I'm protective over Gabby, especially after all Parker put her through these last nine months. Hell, I'm the one who pushed her to get out into the dating world again. I can't fault either of you for your relationship," Christina said, folding her arms across her chest.

Landon appreciated her sentiment. Like himself, Christina and Jacob cared about Gabby. Jacob was the baby's uncle, and it was something Landon would need to accept. The only thing that scared him was the moment Parker returned; because no doubt about it, he'd eventually come to Nano Springs again. It may not be soon, or even ten years from now, but Landon knew he wouldn't stay gone forever.

Chapter Thirteen

The sun peaked in the sky signaling the lunch hour was near. Gabby sighed, gazing around at the beautiful scenery before her. The dock where she stood held so many memories; some good, some heartbreakingly horrific. A bittersweet place that pulled directly at her heartstrings. She'd come outside for a breath of fresh air, having been on bedrest for two weeks since coming home from the hospital with the baby.

Landon had been amazing with the two of them; his patience and love showing beyond leaps and bounds. He was smitten with their daughter and spent every moment he could with them both. It felt weird calling the baby *their* daughter, but she didn't regret her decisions surrounding the baby's birth. Saying *yes* to Landon a few weeks ago was the best decision she'd made for herself and their daughter.

Gabby tugged at her shirt; a size larger than normal but still couldn't cover the kangaroo type pouch she still sported. She couldn't wait to get out of her sweatpants and laughed quietly to herself for how ironic her life had become. When she first became pregnant, she vowed to Christina she'd never be caught wearing the messy mom bun and sweats. But, here she was, standing on the dock in the middle of the day, wearing lounge wear. So much changes when you have a baby.

Checking her watch, she turned to the Inn. When she left earlier, Landon was feeding the baby her bottle and getting her ready for a nap. She wanted to say goodbye before she needed to meet Scarlett at the diner for lunch.

An hour later she pulled into the parking lot at Lizette's. Inside the small diner, decked out in fifty's decor sat Scarlett. She had her purse on the seat next to her at their favorite table, dressed in her Sunday best. Parker's mother would never be caught dead in a messy bun.

"Hello, dear. Motherhood is becoming you."

Gabby beamed. "I never imagined I'd be this relaxed as a mom, but it's so freeing."

"You do look a little pale, have you been eating well?" Scarlett placed the back of her hand against Gabby's forehead.

"Yes, but I'm also being drained regularly by a tiny human, so it's to be expected."

The two ordered their food and gossiped like mother and daughter. Gabby loved the fact that despite Parker's departure from her life, she didn't lose Scarlett in the aftermath. In the days since Gabby came home, she'd vaguely thought of her baby's biological father. Landon helped her forget that she once cried over someone who could abandon her.

"Christina tells me there may be the possibility of a double wedding in the near future, is that true?"

Gabby hesitated. She didn't know where Scarlett was heading with this line of questioning, and the lump that formed in her throat kept her from responding. Would she lose her relationship with Scarlett after all?

"It's okay, child. I'm happy for you."

Gabby sighed and smiled. "When Parker didn't come home after I saw him in L.A., I knew we were done. Landon is not a rebound. He's a little broken like me, but we've spent the past six months healing one another, together. I love him and he's so good with the baby."

"Parker still refuses to answer my calls. Every time I do call, I get that dreadful woman and she never patches him through," Scarlett said, wiping her mouth with a napkin. "I support your decision, and know you never have to worry about judgement from me."

The rest of the lunch went smoothly, and Gabby couldn't wait to get home to her new little family. When she parked at the Inn and walked into her bedroom, she found Landon with Ember laying on his chest. He smiled as she reached down and picked up the baby. Gabby placed a gentle kiss on her forehead before placing her in the bassinet beside the bed.

They chose the name Ember as a homage to the nurse who dedicated hours caring for both herself and the baby. Emberly would always have a place in Gabby's heart.

"How did it go?" Landon asked, stretching his arms above his head.

Gabby lay down beside him and whispered, "I love you." She knew she didn't need to say anything more than that. Even she noticed how content she sounded with their life now.

Landon brushed the hair away from her forehead. Gabby closed her eyes, exhausted, and drained from the day's events, as his arms wrapped around her body. He kissed her lips, her neck, and her lips again. "I love you too, Gabby."

They lay there on the bed until she heard Ember stir in the bassinet. "I'll get her," Gabby said, untangling herself from Landon's embrace.

As she pulled her dress together in her hands to stand up,

she felt her stomach clench and noticed the pool of blood gathering between her legs. Gabby gripped Landon's arms and moaned, as her chin landed firmly on her chest. The room spun. It took two quick heartbeats for her to realize something was seriously, very wrong.

Chapter Fourteen

Parker pulled a cigarette from the pack on the dashboard, as a tune blared from the radio. He'd taken to listening to pop music when in the car alone since Sasha hated the genre of music. The woman had been a thorn in his side since their first meeting over eight months ago, though every now and then her comfort offered something he didn't know he was missing.

The engine of his black Jeep Wrangler reeved angry as he accelerated down sunny Rodeo Drive. The sun burned against his tanned skin. Glancing in the rearview mirror at his reflection, no one would be able to tell he hailed from Vermont. Sometimes he missed home when he let himself think of his life there. He missed Gabby. Some days he wondered how her life was turning out without him. Had she moved on?

Palm trees passed in a blur along the road to his two-bedroom condo. The jeep he'd purchased with his first paycheck from the T.V pilots he'd landed over the last few months, fit four but most days he rode alone.

Sasha joined him for dinner every now and then, but those dates were for appearances. It was part of his deal with her; join him in public at important events, share a few kisses, and she'd talk to her producer friend to help with his career. Without her, he'd already have gone home with his head down, shame written in marker across his face.

Parker thought back to the day he attempted to make a phone call to Gabby, he'd used an untraceable phone. He wasn't even supposed to call, it was part of the deal he'd made with Sasha. The day they agreed to be partners, he cut off his phone service and ditched the cell in a trash can outside his hotel. Sasha made him believe that Gabby was better off without him, especially now that he was slowly making a name for himself. It took months for him to secure the phone to call his Mom. Sasha wasn't too cold to keep him from doing that, but still she monitored his calls. In her twisted mind, she was protecting him from giving up a life she believed he could find success with. He may as well not even have the phone. Parker banged a fist on the dashboard; damn himself to hell for letting her control him.

Once he made it home, Parker pulled the key to the condo from his blue jeans pocket and turned it in the lock. The moment he stepped into the place and removed his jacket, he knew something was amiss. He wasn't alone. Reaching for the baseball bat he kept by the front door, he positioned it on his shoulder and stepped from the entryway into the living room.

"Hey! Bro," Jacob said, stepping from the kitchen. He held a beer from the fridge and stopped at the counter. "Long time, no see."

His casualness annoyed Parker, who was immediately on guard. What brought his brother all the way to L.A.? "How did you find me?" Parker asked, setting the bat against the white leather sofa. Jacob had become a solid man in less than a year. He sported a new dark beard, his hair was trimmed close to his head, and were those frown lines around his eyes?

Jacob placed the beer on the counter and shoved his hands

in the pockets of his brown leather jacket. Parker gave it to him for his last birthday, a day that was much happier than the one they were dealing with now. Jacob's grey flannel shirt put him out of place in the white walled condo.

"Dude, are you serious?" Jacob folded his arms over his chest, they too had changed and were thicker than Parker remembered.

"Ten months and all you can say to me is, 'how did you find me?', I should have known." Jacob scoffed.

Before Parker could respond, Jacob turned to the window that overlooked the hills to the East. Parker wasn't sure if he should respond so he leaned against the wall and waited. Clearly Jacob had something on his mind.

Sasha stepped through the front door before Jacob could say anything. Instead, he scoffed, and Parker cringed at Sasha's timing.

"Who's this?" Sasha asked, wrapping her arm around Parker's waist. "You didn't tell me we were having company."

"Jacob meet Sasha, Sasha, meet my brother Jacob."

Jacob ignored the hand Sasha offered.

It felt like eternity before Jacob finally spoke. When he did, his voice choked, and Parker realized he was fighting back tears. Growing up, Jacob rarely cried. Always wanted to act the tough guy, never wanting to appear weak even if he were the younger brother. The dampness of his eyes put a fear in Parker he never experience before.

"Is it Mom?" Parker asked, wanting to comfort his brother. When Jacob turned to face him, he thought better of it. Anger radiated through Jacob's eyes.

"No, it's not Mom. She's hurting, but only because of you."

Parker sighed with relief, but it was short lived.

Jacob roughly brushed away at the tears forming in his eyes, revealing the anger laced within them. "It's Gabby. Parker, she's dead."

PARKER FOUGHT the urge to take another glance at his brother seated in the airplane seat beside him, hours after listening to his brother tell him his worst nightmare.

The news Jacob dropped on him four hours before took time to process; time he hadn't been allowed. Losing his nerve, he tried to offer a small smile at his brother, encouragement since Jacob had never flown in a private jet before. To be truthful, neither had Parker. This would be the first time. Jacob's eyes narrowed as he adjusted himself in his seat and reached for the glass of whiskey on the table beside him.

The hum of the engine purred beneath them as the Cessna Citation XLS came to life and began its journey down the runway. Sasha made her way from the cockpit after speaking with the pilot. "I've instructed the pilot to make stops in both Texas and Tennessee for fill ups. We'll need to stretch our legs anyway," she said, buckling herself into the seat next to Parker.

He didn't want her to join them on the trip to Nano Springs, but she wouldn't take no for an answer. Sasha pretended not to hear him when he said tension would be high in his hometown and instructed their bags to be sent over to the airport straight away. To Jacob's credit, he kept his mouth closed but the constant eye rolls and deep sighs told Parker everything he needed to know about Jacob's disapproval.

While Sasha was busy preparing the jet, Parker tried to explain his relationship with the woman, but Jacob turned away and shut him out. Sasha was many things; annoying, persistent, and high maintenance, but she also saved his ass when it came to his time in L.A., more times than he could count. If it weren't for her connections between the music and film industry he wouldn't have made it as far as he had in his career.

Every time he thought about going home, Sasha reminded him how much Gabby would resent him for being gone if he didn't make a bigger name for himself. "What would all the heartbreak of you leaving put her through if you went home with nothing to show for it?" Sasha had a way of manipulating him, something he didn't realize until it was too late.

Jacob seemed to have no interest in any explanation he'd offered to give, so he gave up. Instead, he reached for Sasha's hand and tried to convince her to stay at the hotel in town while he took care of things back home. Even if no one else had any interest in his visit, Parker needed to see his mother. He couldn't change his relationship with Gabby, but at least he could reconcile with Scarlett.

Parker gazed at the scenery outside the tiny plane window. The clouds parted as the plane began its rise to 30,000 feet. As far as planes went, he couldn't complain of comfort. The soft leather seats and privacy was a large cry from his flight ten months ago. There were no screaming kids, no sick people who refused to stay home but instead coughed their mucus all over their seatmates.

Yeah, this was the life.

As he allowed his mind to wander back to the last day he held Gabby in his arms, Parker was finally able to release the built-up grief he'd been keeping inside. Even when Sasha reached over to squeeze his hand, all he could picture was Gabby. What had he done? Better yet, how had she died? He knew asking Jacob for details could likely set the dude off again, so he opted for a show of sympathy.

"Gabby's parents must be beside themselves," he said, turning to face his brother. The plane shifted, as if unhappy with his statement, and he could feel the bile start to climb in his throat.

"There's so much you don't know, and I'm not sure if you deserve to know," Jacob said, placing the empty glass on the table with a clink. "Actually, maybe I should tell you, then you'll know what fresh hell you put Gabby though by not being around."

"Now wait a minute," Sasha said, sitting forward in her seat. Her eyebrows creased as she surveyed the two of them. "Parker was following his dream. Gabby couldn't hold that against him. He was coming back."

"I think you should tell your little girlfriend to butt out. If I wasn't in such a hurry to get back to my fiancée I would have taken a commercial flight."

Jacob was engaged? Wow! There was a lot he didn't know.

"Take it easy, both of you. Jacob, I don't want to play this pull and tug game with you all the way back to Vermont. Just tell me what happened."

"Gabby's parents were killed in a freak Labor Day accident in front of Gabby and the whole town." Jacob's deadened toned reminded Parker of someone who had the life drained out of them. How could he be so cold and hollow. Couldn't he know this was hard for Parker to hear?

Sasha gasped. "That sounds so horrific, losing a whole family in less than a year," she said, her hand resting over her heart.

Parker knew she was being dramatic, and her little jabs at how ridiculous he was being was starting to piss him off. Maybe it was time to cut ties with her after they got to Nano Springs. It wasn't as if they both didn't know they were using each other.

"Good Lord," Jacob said, pulling a baseball cap from the backpack at his feet. "Wake me when we've landed in Nano Springs."

The rest of the flight passed without any excitement, and for that Parker was thankful. Though, Sasha yapping at clients over the phone nearly unnerved him to no end. Why did he have such a difficult time saying no to the woman?

Night had fallen when the wheels finally touched down on the short tarmac outside of Nano Springs. The moon hung high surrounded by a dozen tiny stars against the warm sky.

Parker gathered his bag and watched as Jacob thanked the pilot before descending the stairs of the plane. He almost asked if they needed to call a cab before he realized Jacob was heading towards an awaiting car.

"Looks like you're one step ahead of us, thanks for calling a ride, man," Parker said, slinging his bag over his shoulder as he jogged towards the car.

Jacob paused and held up his hand. He'd opened the passenger side door, his arms slung over the top. "Believe me, you don't want to get into a moving car with Cristina anytime soon."

Leaving Parker with his mouth hanging open, Jacob ducked into the car and the driver sped away without a second thought.

PARKER RELISHED in the moment of silence later that night in the motel bathroom. The rooms at Nano Inn weren't what he'd been accustomed to since arriving in L.A., but they'd do for the short visit home. The longer he stayed in Nano Springs, knowing he couldn't see or even try to reconnect with Gabby, the more he realized he couldn't stay there without her. He winced as the lock clicked on the bathroom door, praying Sasha wouldn't wake up. He needed some time to let go and grief before he faced the others in the morning.

His relationship with Sasha over the last few months had grown from being friends, to business partners. Parker hadn't slept with her, because a small part of him knew he'd never have a chance of reconnecting with Gabby if he did, but the two shared a kiss or two for the public. Parker would have had to master the art of groveling even with the intimacy they'd shared, but now he supposed he was off the hook. Which was a horrible thought to have at that moment. He'd rather be groveling.

As the bathroom fan switched on and began its annoying hum, Parker lay his head in his hands and silently sobbed. It was the first time since they'd arrived that he could mourn the loss of the only women he'd ever loved. Why did he have to be so stupid? Gabby was everything for him; kind, loving, and compassionate.

He wondered how the last few months of her life was like, besides her parent's death. That couldn't have been easy. At least she had Christina and Jacob, it seemed. His brother seemed mighty protective of Gabby. Had something happened between the two? Parker stood in front of the bathroom sink, the water running slow from the faucet. Nah, he wouldn't be engaged if Gabby was anything more than a friend.

"Ugh," he said, silently. Christina wasn't someone he was looking forward to seeing the next day. Christina and Gabby had been friends for years, and he had seen Christina's wrath a time or two. The woman could make hell for anyone who hurt the ones she loved. Maybe tomorrow wouldn't be a good idea to see her, a visit to his mother's seemed like a safer option.

His Mother. What was he supposed to say to her? He knew she tried to call a few times but each phone call was blocked by Sasha, as he auditioned for one show and another. Leaving his mother wasn't something he regretted because not only did she have Jacob around, but Scarlett was constantly traveling for her own career as an author.

The fan in the bathroom started to give him a headache. He quickly splashed cold water on his face, mentally reminding himself to shave in the morning. Turning off the light, he stepped into the double queen bedroom and stripped down to his boxers. He cast a glance at Sasha and contemplated slipping between the covers next to her. Thinking better of the idea, he pulled back the comforter and laid down, impressed by the softness of the mattress.

Parker threw his arm above his head, wrapping it over to his opposite shoulder. He stared at the popcorn ceiling and considered his options for the following day. There wasn't anything he could do for Gabby, besides go visit the gravesite. After he had lunch at his mother's house, per a text from Jacob once they reached the motel, he'd stop and say goodbye to the girlfriend he left behind. As his eyes drooped closed, he wondered if he'd ever feel the same way about another woman. Did he even deserve to have the kind of love Gabby offered him, at all?

THE NEXT MORNING, Parker opened his eyes to the sight of Sasha, her expression hopeful, standing over him with a to-go cup of coffee in her hand. Her red hair was already styled, and her make up painted on. She didn't do things halfway, even when traveling out of town. That was one thing he liked about her; professionalism didn't go away just because she wasn't at work. Her sundress was the only thing that set her apart from how she appeared. Of course, Vermont in summer, a sundress was ideal.

He sat up, resting his bare back against the headboard. "Thanks, I didn't sleep well last night. Coffee is just what I need right now," he said, reaching for the cup.

Confused, he wasn't sure what to make out of her jerking the coffee away from his reach.

"Oh, sweetheart, this isn't for you. I tried to wake you before I left to grab breakfast, but you wouldn't budge. I have your breakfast over there," she said, motioning behind her on the dresser. "You were in such a deep sleep; I almost didn't want to wake you. But we need to talk."

Four words a woman could say that buckled a man at his knees: *we need to talk*. He took a deep breath and straightened in the bed, letting one-foot fall to the floor. Parker leaned forward and patted the edge of the bed. Sasha sat down, tucking her dress under her bottom.

They were scheduled to meet his mother for lunch at eleven, so they'd have to make the conversation a quick one.

"I agree. I've done a lot of thinking in the last twenty-four hours." He started to launch into his speech when she pressed her polished finger against his lips.

"I meant, I needed to say something. Let me go first." Sasha placed the cup of coffee on the end table.

Parker tried everything he could not to imagine the hot liquid pouring down his throat. Instead, he sat back against the headboard, his arms folded across his chest. No matter what she said, he knew how he felt and this time his gut wasn't telling him he was making a big mistake. This time, he knew he couldn't stay in Nano Springs. The memories alone would kill him. Gabby had been a huge part of his life, being back in town only reminded him of how much he failed her.

Sasha was talking and he shut off his own inner voice and listened to what she had to say.

"I need to know if you're done with L.A., because if you are then we can work with that. I know it makes me seem like the most horrible person in the world, but I'm ready for a change myself. I want to make that change with you, Parker." Her words were rushed, as if he'd say no and crush her spirit.

There wasn't anything keeping them in Nano Springs. Parker suddenly had the urge to leave the area. "Listen, I have something I need to do before we head to my mom's for lunch.

Why don't you stay here and pack up, and I'll be back shortly to get you? We'll go have lunch at mom's, let her interrogate you, and then we'll go back to California to settle our business there. After that, the sky is the limit."

Sasha may be annoying and manipulative, but that determination would get her far. Gabby was gone. If he was honest with himself, as much as Sasha annoyed him, she'd had her moments that grew on him the last few months. It was his own disappointment in himself that put up the wall that kept her at arm's length. Maybe now was a chance to make a change.

"I'd love that," Sasha said, standing and walking over to her purse. With her back to him, she pulled out her cellphone and began dialing numbers. "It's time for you to put your old life to rest." As if realizing how insensitive she may be, she turned with the phone to her ear and offered a small smile. "I'm really sorry that this is how it came about."

Parker rose to shower and before he stepped into the bathroom, he wrapped his arms around her and kissed her neck. He knew being alone wasn't something he could deal with right now, and who knows what the future held. He grieved for Gabby the night before, he'll grieve for her many more nights to come. That didn't mean he had to stop life in its tracks. He nuzzled Sasha's neck and whispered the worlds most cheesiest lines, "Second chances are life's greatest gifts," he said, brushing his lips over her shoulder before stepping away.

Once he showered, dressed, and gave Sasha another kiss, Parker reeved up the economy rental car and headed towards Nano Springs Cemetery. Saying a final goodbye to Gabby and the life they shared together wouldn't be easy for him. It may seem like he was moving on, but he and Gabby were over the moment he stepped on the plane to Hollywood. It took finding out she died and the many tears he sobbed in the motel bathroom for him to realize that.

After a short drive, he pulled the rental into the parking lot next to a familiar black SUV. If he didn't know any better he'd think Gabby wasn't dead and his brother was playing an awfully cruel joke on him. Unless someone else had gotten the same model vehicle, it was Gabby's. The license plate confirmed it.

As he stepped from the rental, the previously cloudy sky opened, and rain fell from the heavens. Such perfect weather to say goodbye. Each headstone was placed seven feet apart unless the deceased were a couple. Parker remembered the night Gabby's parents shared their plans for pre-purchasing plots. "It's morbid," she cried. In the same sentence though she told him she wanted to be buried right beside her parents.

When he asked her about being buried together, Gabby shrugged her shoulders and said, "My parents will never break up with me, leave me. Boyfriends and Girlfriends don't have any binding ties to each other." He argued that things would be different when they married and all she could do was laugh and say, "well, let's revisit this conversation once you've put a ring on my finger."

At the memory, he rubbed his hands over his empty ring finger. Maybe it was her lack of faith in their relationship that helped seal the deal of him going after the acting dream. He shook his head; blaming her for his faults was something a loser would do, and he felt like the biggest one.

Gabby's parents' plots were in the middle of the cemetery. The artificial grass was pretty, but it didn't do anyone any favors when it got drenched with rainwater. His tennis shoes were soaked by the time he stepped four feet into the cemetery. Parker noticed a figure standing near where the Lawson's gravesite would be, and he could feel the hairs on the back of his neck stand up.

As he got closer, he noticed the man held an umbrella and cursed himself for not thinking to bring one of his own. By the time he reached the gravesite in front of Gabby's parents plot, the rain had settled into a drizzle, so at least someone above was watching over him. The man wore faded blue jeans, work boots, and a black windbreaker that was soaked to the bone despite the umbrella.

Parker wanted to say hello and as he raised his hand, he froze. The guy stood in front of Gabby's grave. The headstone read her full name: *Gabriella Marie Lawson*, (good, she hadn't married), and her date of birth and death. Underneath the dates an inscription he was having trouble reading caught his attention. *Loving daughter, friend, fiancée, and mother.*

Mother? Fiancée? Parker couldn't believe it. Gabby had a child while he was gone? This didn't make any sense. He tried to turn and walk away but paused when he heard the smallest cry he'd ever heard. Just then, the man turned and stumbled, having been startled by a drenched Parker.

The man wore a 49ers ball cap over wavy blonde locks; rain dripped onto a pink blanket. It was then that Parker realized the man had a fabric carrier strapped to his chest. The man put a protective hand against the baby's back and began to back away. Who was this guy? The fiancé?

"I'm...Um, how do you know Gabby?" Parker tried to sound casual but like with most else in his life, he failed. His voice shook, though he couldn't be sure if it was of freight or anger.

The man didn't response right away, though Parker did notice his eyes travel up and down his body once. He had a look of disgust on his face like Parker had never seen before. Had to be the fiancé.

Finally, after what seemed like forever, the man spoke. "Hello, Parker. I'm Landon, Gabby's fiancé."

Chapter Fifteen

L andon thought losing Gabby would end him, and if it weren't for Ember, he probably wouldn't be standing in front of Gabby's grave. He'd be buried beside her. The day she started bleeding, was one of the worst days of their lives. It took four pints of blood and her heart stopping twice for her to be stable enough to move to the ICU. Even then, it wasn't enough.

Gabby fought hard, but in the end, the tear after her delivery had ripped open and depilated her blood supply and energy. The doctors called her time of death early the next morning. Landon was dumbfounded. How one minute they could be discussing their future together, to her laying cold in his arms.

By the look on Parker's face in the graveyard, no one told him about the baby. He stood there, looking like a drowned dog, his mouth gaping open like he'd seen a ghost. If he weren't still grieving, the sight would be hilarious. The guy deserved the shock of his life. Too bad it took Gabby dying for him to get what was coming to him.

Landon watched as Parker sputtered and took a step backwards. All the while, Landon put a firm hand on Ember's back, not wanting to fight with the baby nearby. He wanted to get her out of the crummy weather, they'd only stopped at the gravesite for their daily chat with Gabby. Landon had taken to bringing her by every day before her nap. It was the only connection she could have with her mother, and he wanted her to have the moment, even if she wouldn't remember it later.

"I don't believe this," Parker said, wiping the water from his fading beard. "I have a daughter?"

If the comment hadn't sent a shock of anger straight threw his chest, he'd almost laugh at the insanity of the man. What did Gabby see in this arrogant piece of shit? The guy had known about the baby for all of one minute before he laid claim to her? *Over my dead body.*

Instead of responding to Parker's preposterous question, Landon pressed two fingers to his lips and touched them to the cold, hard stone of Gabby's grave without taking his eyes off of the man before him. "Goodbye, my love. We'll see you tomorrow." Without another glance at Parker, he turned and walked away.

Landon had recognized the scumbag right away; from the pictures he'd found when he and Christina went through Gabby's things. Of course, in those photographs the crow's feet and shaded beard didn't exist. Gabby would be happy to see Parker had aged since those photos were taken.

"Hey! Wait up! We're not done here." Parker rushed up beside him, placing his hand on Landon's shoulder.

With a hard shrug, Landon removed his hand and turned to face him. "I have nothing else to say to you. Have questions? I'm sure your mother would be happy to answer them." Without another word he made his way quickly to the car, the slosh of water soaking his shoes. He'd need to hang up his socks when he got back to the room.

As he pulled Ember from the carrier, he heard the car next to him reeved up and peel from the parking lot. Ember's body jolted once before settling into a much needed nap. Landon took a moment to gaze at the infant's face, her lashes longer than some women's. Her pouty lips puckered in her sleep, and his heart melted all over again.

The car seat belt clicked into place and Landon gently shut the door. If there were no sudden disturbances, Ember would sleep all the way through her naptime. Once in the driver seat, he pulled out his cellphone and dialed Christina's number. She'd become a good friend since Gabby's death, a notion that surprised him. Maybe he'd earned her respect, but between Christina and Jacob, he'd managed to survive losing Gabby, especially in the days after her death. The three of them leaned on one another.

"Chris, hey! Yeah, Ember is fine," he said, glancing at the car seat in the rear-view mirror. "Can you meet me at the Inn though? I just met Parker Warrick."

Christina sighed, as if she expected such news. Did she know Parker was in town? Of course, Jacob *was* his brother. They were bound to know by now. "We're supposed to meet Parker and his new girlfriend at Scarlett's, but Jacob can do this one alone," she said. "Meet you in ten?"

"Wow! A girlfriend? I didn't expect that. Yeah, ten minutes will work. See you soon."

The call dropped and Landon placed the cell phone in the cup holder. He wondered how Parker's new girlfriend will take the news Parker was sure to share with her. Well, it really didn't matter. No one was taking Ember from him.

Christina was his rock after Gabby's death. Jacob too. Landon was blown away by the way the two stepped up. Put their differences aside, considering he wasn't family, and helped out.

The log cabin he'd purchased was down the road from Jacob's own cabin was a surprise he'd purchased before Gabby died. Both places were getting upgrades and maintenance done, so the couple and Landon took rooms at the Inn until they were ready. Christina and Jacob being right across the hall worked perfectly for all involved. Their closeness helped Landon with the grieving, and once, Christina said he'd helped her as well.

Once Ember was settled in her crib back at the Inn, Landon grabbed the white baby monitor and crossed the hall to Christina and Jacob's room. The baby monitor only had sound as Gabby said she heard too many horror stories about ghosts and paranormal figures popping up on those video monitors. She'd insisted on the ones they had, and Landon wasn't going against her, even if she weren't there anymore.

When Christina opened the door, she offered a small smile and ushered him inside. "How's our princess?"

Landon raised the monitor and said, "snoozing like a logger sawing wood." They both chuckled as they sat down together on the sofa. Christina and Jacob's room mirrored Landon and Ember's. Same rustic design and furniture, though their window overlooked the parking lot as his once did, before he moved in with Gabby.

"So, how was it? I haven't seen him yet. Well, unless you count through the car windshield when I picked Jacob up from the airport last night." Christina crossed her legs under her and placed her hands in her lap. Before he'd even responded, he saw her twisting her t-shirt in her hands.

"Short and sweet. He automatically tried to lay claim on the baby and said nothing about Gabby. Did anyone tell him about Ember?"

"No. Scarlett refused to talk to him until the lunch today," Christina said, checking her watch, "or, lunch right now, I guess.

136

Jacob said he only told his brother about Gabby's death. Not the how or why, or anything about Ember."

Landon heard a blip on the monitor, but nothing came after, so he turned his attention back to Christina. "Wait! Jacob went to California? Why?"

Christina stood up and paced the floor. Landon could tell she was nervous, and he didn't blame her. Parker coming back into the picture, no matter how much legal security they had with Ember, could cause problems. Issues neither wanted to have to deal with so soon after Gabby's death.

"You can't be mad at him. Scarlett convinced him that Parker deserved to know about Gabby's death. But, we haven't had a phone number for him in months, unless you count the number that his girlfriend controlled. Jacob went out to L.A. and asked around, at that point he wasn't too hard to find. Apparently, he scored on the career front, though nothing big named to go national."

Landon sat back on the sofa, soaking in all the new information. He couldn't fault Jacob and would never ask him to choose sides between Landon and his own mother. Though, Landon still didn't understand why Scarlett would insist on Parker knowing.

There was another blip on the monitor and then a bigger one as he heard the door slam from the hallway. In a matter of seconds he jerked open the door and rushed over to his room. His gut dropped a few centimeters as he peered over the crib. Inside lay Ember's stuffed lamb, her covers tossed to the side. Ember was gone.

THE POLICE STOOD in the hallway, whispering to one another. Landon paced the room with Jacob and Christina on the sofa watching his every move. He would be out there

137

hunting Parker down if the police weren't guarding the door. It angered him that they wouldn't let him join the search.

"I thought your brother was supposed to be at lunch with you!" Landon stopped in front of Jacob. To his credit, Jacob looked remorseful. His head dropped to his chest in defeat.

"Parker called, ranting, and yelling about how we'd withheld information from him and that by not telling him about the baby, we'd chosen our side. Mother is beside herself and feels guilty for even asking me to bring him back here. Parker never showed up to the lunch and I was about to call Christina when your call came in."

Landon continued pacing and then paused at the window overlooking the lake. Anger filled his eyes at the thought of how frightened Ember would be without him. If Parker was as angry as Jacob described him, who knew what he'd do. Landon couldn't just sit here and do nothing. He had to find Ember.

"Christina, I know I promised you I wouldn't leave with Ember. But I can't stay here if he's here. I can't keep being scared he'll do this again. When we find my daughter, she and I will be on the first flight out of here."

Landon grabbed his jacket and stepped out the door. "I have to go check on some issue downstairs with the Inn," he said, hoping they wouldn't see through his bluff. When he promised to be right back, they let him go.

The sound of gravel sputtering under the tires of the SUV a minute later, was like fuel on a raging fire. Landon headed down the long gravel road to Main Street, his eyes blazing with worry and anger. The clouds had cleared, and the sun was fighting hard to come out and play. As he turned onto Main Street his phone chirped with a new text.

Jacob: *Try the Nano Springs Motel at the South end of town. I'm really sorry about all of this. Please don't leave town.*

We'll get you through this.

Landon dropped the cellphone and sped towards the motel. Once he arrived, he spotted the car that had parked next to him at the cemetery, sitting in front of room number five. Landon blocked the car with his own and left the motor running. Within seconds, he was pounding on the door. From where he stood, he could hear Ember crying hard inside. The sound ripped his heart and caused him to pound even more. He'd break the door down if they didn't open it soon.

A red-headed woman opened the door, the chain still attached. "What do you want?" she said, glancing behind her.

"Let me in. Where's Parker? I wanna speak to the bastard who had the nerve to steal a sleeping baby from her crib."

When the woman didn't let him in, Landon couldn't take listening to Ember's cry's any longer. He'd have to come pay old man Davis for the busted chain. The crack in the wood sounded like victory as he burst into the room. The woman fell back against the wall and braced herself to stand.

"You can't be in here!" Her screams were ignored as Landon lifted Ember from the bed and looked quickly around for Parker.

"Tell Parker that if he ever lays another hand on my daughter, he'd wish he never came back to Nano Springs."

Holding Ember tightly to his chest, he rushed to the car and quickly buckled her into the seat. Just as he peeled away from the motel, he saw Parker walking back from the motel shop, a bag of diapers under his arm.

Landon knew he couldn't go back to the Inn so he went to the only other place he could think of; the cabin. The tress blurred by as he fumbled with his cellphone. He searched for Christina's number as he made the turn down the dirt road that would lead to the cut off between their cabins.

"Christina. I have Ember. We're going to the cabin. Meet

me there if you want but try and make sure you aren't followed. The last place I want them is our cabin."

Ember began to fuss again in the backseat, and he tried to calm her by singing. It was something Gabby did in the early days after her birth. Once Ember's cries turned to whimpers, Landon dialed Christina's number again. "Bring Lamby."

The phone disconnected as he turned the car into the driveway. A log cabin stood on the two-acre property. It wasn't completely ready for them to move in, but he could make do until he figured out his next move. He hoped Christina would think to bring supplies, though he had diapers and formula already at the cabin. Landon could go without for days, but he'd be damned if he let his daughter starve.

Landon carried the entire car seat into the cabin with a now sleeping Ember resting inside. Thankfully the lights were connected, and they had running water. To be honest, they could move in if it weren't for the driveway being unfinished. He hadn't wanted the construction noise to keep Ember awake but after the events of the day, things may need to change.

What on earth was he going to do about Parker? He couldn't believe the guy would outright steal the baby. The guy must have gone mad in whatever little bit of grief he'd managed to conjure up. Not to mention the girl he'd come with; were they so close that she'd help him commit a felony?

The sound of an engine put Landon on high alert as he placed Ember on the couch by the door. Looking between the blinds, he recognized Christina dark blue SUV immediately. A sigh of relief escaped between his lips as he opened the door. She rushed in and made a beeline for Ember's carrier.

"Oh, sweet baby! I'm so glad your daddy got you back safely."

"Christina, what am I going to do now?" Landon sat next to Ember's carrier. He grabbed Lamby from Christina and placed it against the side of Ember's head. "I can't hide from this dude forever."

"Deep breaths," she said, patting his arm. "Jacob is beside himself but knows the right thing to do is contact his buddy who's a lawyer here in town. The guy knew Parker too, growing up, but he despises what Parker did to Gabby. Besides, the guy is by the book. Jacob is showing him the birth certificate and everything. We'll get this sorted out."

Landon rested his head against the back of the leather couch. His eyes closed, he asked, "Even the letter?"

"Yes. Landon, you have to be thankful Gabby even wrote that letter. A birth certificate has a good chance of holding up in court, but a letter from the mother? Even stronger."

Landon found the letter two weeks after Gabby died. He was sorting through the drawer beside their bed one night, searching for any kind of sleeping aid that would give him a moments rest. Stuck between a small bible and her journal for Ember, was a handwritten letter from Gabby. Landon read that letter twenty times that night, and then shared it with Christina and Jacob the following day. Without the letter, he didn't think Jacob would ever accept him as Ember's father.

"Let's hope it works," he said, opening his eyes as Ember stirred beside him. She opened her tiny green eyes and scrunched her face up, prepared to cry. Before things could get out of hand, he unbuckled the belts and picked her up and placed her on his chest.

"It's okay, little one. Daddy's here."

They sat in silence, Landon lost in thoughts about the life he'd have to live without Gabby. A chirp vibrated from Christina's pocket, bringing Landon back to the present. Ember's head began the searching motion she did when she was hungry.

"I'm going to get her a bottle while you answer your phone," he said, carrying Ember into the kitchen. As he warmed the water, he overheard Christina in the other room.

"Well, I suppose that's the best we can hope for."

When he walked back into the living room, Ember laying in his arms sucking from the bottle, he looked hopeful at Christina. She was placing her phone in her pocket and smiled when he settled onto the couch.

"You have a meeting with Judge Bayer first thing in the morning. You'll plead your case, Parker will plead his and then the judge will make the ruling. You can keep Ember tonight, and dumbass will spend the night in jail for the kidnapping. Those are charges he may face later, but for now we need to put this issue to rest."

Landon had to admit, he was shocked Parker wasn't getting a more severe punishment, but he was thankful they could rest easy for the night. "What about his girlfriend, she was an accomplice, wasn't she?"

"According to Jacob, she posted her own bail. They wouldn't allow her to post Parker's."

"Great, just when I thought we were all safe."

Christina stood and gathered her purse. "Don't worry Landon. Between me, the cop sitting outside now, and Jacob, I assure you, rest easy tonight."

Landon thanked her for her help and told her to thank Jacob as well. He knew it couldn't be easy to go against your own brother. Once Christina drove away, Landon spotted the patrol car near the mailbox at the end of the wooded drive. Regardless of the protective measures in place, he knew he'd never sleep.

As he prepared Ember for bed, changing her into her footed pajamas and singing her bedtime song, he wondered what the next day would hold for them both. Would tonight be the last night he'd sing her the bedtime song?

With Ember snug in her crib, Landon planted himself in the

white rocking chair near the bed. A soft lamp gave him a glimpse of her tiny body, as he rocked back and forth, humming the tune of the song he sung every night to lull her to sleep.

Tomorrow they would rise and dress in their best clothes. He'd get her ready and they'd head to the courthouse.

Tomorrow he'd fight for his right to be in her life.

Chapter Sixteen

Parker woke on the hard surface called a bed in the Nano Springs Jail the next morning. He couldn't believe a lot of things but getting ready for a custody hearing in an hour was at the top of the list. Why hadn't Gabby told him she was pregnant? He winced as the sunlight poured through the tiny, barred window in the left corner of the small cell. Was that what she'd come to L.A. for all those months ago?

He began to pace the cell as thousands of questions bombarded his brain. There was so much that he didn't understand, most of all how he not only had a daughter, but some other guy was raising her. Jacob played his cards last night and showed him what an ugly hand he had for his brother. It shouldn't surprise him; the younger Warrick was always weak when it came to women. Naturally, he'd follow whatever Christina told him to do.

Mid-stride to the wall, Parker heard the buzz of the door opening at the end of the hall. He couldn't wait to get out of the musty smelling jailhouse and into fresh air again. Spending the night in jail only angered him further. What kind of law enforcement arrested a man for taking his own child?

When he glanced up at the figure standing in front of his cell, his face immediately brightened. "Sasha, oh baby I'm so glad to see you."

"Parker, you look terrible. Listen, I only stopped by to drop off this suit, so you'd have a chance at winning this thing. But I didn't sign up to be a mom. When we talked yesterday, you said you were ready to wrap up this chapter of your life. Now you're fighting for custody of a kid?"

"Sasha, please. Babe, I can't turn my back on my own daughter."

She placed her hands on her hips. In that moment, she looked ten years younger. "Damn, Parker. Until twelve hours ago you didn't even know you had a daughter."

Parker gripped the bars and placed his face against the cool rungs. "I have to see this through. We can figure things out after that."

Sasha hung the hanger on the bar and pressed her lips to his. "I'll see you at the hearing. Being in a relationship may be your only hope at winning."

Parker breathed a sigh of relief as an officer approached the cell and let him out. Sasha left to go to the courthouse, promising him she'd be there waiting. It took all of an hour to change, splash cold water on his face, and get to the courthouse by way of police car. The criminal look didn't suit him, and it didn't help that the whole community seemed to show up outside the steps of the courthouse. He knew without asking none of them were there to support him.

The courthouse was small, but the stairs leading up to it were massive. Parker passed through the security with no issues and was ushered into the judge's chambers right at nine o'clock. As he stepped through the door, he noticed the man, Landon, standing behind a small table in front of the judge's desk.

Parker took his place at the other table and waited. The only people allowed in the room were Parker and Landon, and any witnesses the judge chose to call and their attorney's. Landon had Parker's old friend, Dawson, while Parker was left with a public defender. It didn't take long for him to realize he had no chance at winning custody of his daughter. Each man was given the chance to make a statement.

"Your honor, I am here today because I was never given any idea that Gabby Lawson was pregnant. Yes, I left town but as far as I knew, our relationship was intact. The child is my biological daughter and I want nothing more than to be her father."

Parker gripped one hand in the other as he braced to hear Landon's statement. Instead, it was the judge who spoke next. "Mr. Warrick, usually I side with the biological parents in cases like these, however I'm troubled by your statement. It is to my knowledge that you ceased communication with not only Ms. Lawson, but your family as well. I think we can all agree that would signify ending a relationship. Not to mention, the "child" is named Ember. Do you not even know that?"

"But Your Honor—," Parker said, stumbling over his words. Even before he could say anything else he felt the fight drain out of him. What she said was true, he admitted that to himself the day before.

"To make things fair, I'd like to hear the statement Mr. Marshall has prepared," the judge said, her glasses falling to the rim of her nose.

Parker closed his eyes and hung his head as he listened to what Landon had to say.

"Minus conception, I have been with Ember her entire life. I'd just met Gabby and a month later found out she was pregnant. When I came here, it was to get away and find purpose. Gabby and I connected on a level I wasn't expecting. We became engaged hours before she went into labor. Before she gave birth, we sealed our commitment to each other by putting my name on the birth certificate. We named her and spent two amazing weeks as a family before Gabby was taken from us. I ask you, please don't take my daughter too."

Landon then turned to Parker and continued. "Parker, I know deep down, Gabby wouldn't want us to fight over the baby. And when Ember grows up, I never want her to think I kept her biological father from her. If you're willing to be a positive influence in her life, I'm open to visitations. But, stealing her? I can't. I know Gabby wouldn't want her raised with that kind of negativity."

Once Landon was done speaking, Parker opened his mouth to speak. "Your Honor, it's clear the outcome here today. If it pleases the court, I'll take my leave now." The sound of the gravel banging against the wood released the grief he didn't realize he had. The level of anger he held towards himself and Sasha for convincing him to stay in L.A. overpowered him. Now he'd have to not only visit a town where the woman he loved no longer existed, but share visitation with a stranger who wasn't even related to his daughter?

The judge released him on probation for the kidnapping charges, though he hardly heard anything after he'd given up. Parker didn't even bother shaking hands with Landon. He turned and left the courthouse and found Sasha waiting near the car out front.

"I'm so sorry Parker, but maybe it's for the best." She must have seen the look of defeat he'd painted on his face.

Parker opened the passenger door for her, and she silently slid into the empty seat. With one last look at the courthouse, he started the car and drove away. His heart drummed inside his chest as images of his life with Gabby flew through his mind like a blur of the passing trees. Sasha droned on in the seat beside him, doing everything but making him feel better.

"You had to know you wouldn't walk out of there with the baby, right?" she asked, turning to face him.

Instead of responding, he gripped the steering wheel until his knuckles were white. The engined purred loudly as he pressed his foot to the floorboard. Parker eyed the final lookout point, a place he'd visited often when he needed to get away, in the distance at the edge of town. Surrounded by maple trees, the bridge sloped down and ran into a small river.

Sasha shouted profanities and gripped the handle above the door. The shrill of her voice excited something dark within him as she yelled at him to slow down. He almost laughed at her use of an imaginary break. A final glance in the rearview mirror, a glimpse of life fading behind him, before he turned the wheel to the right, causing the car to go off the road. The thumping of the tires on the marks on the edge of the road told him to readjust, but he didn't.

The car raced at top speed right into the riverbank clipping its front fender into a nearby tree. Water rushed into the car, wiping away the blood from the crack both his and Sasha's heads made against the windshield. Before darkness overtook him Parker thought, *guilt kills people too.*

Epilogue

On the way home from the courthouse, Ember happily chewed on Lamby as if she too could sense the relief that filled Landon's heart. She was starting to find her voice, and her squeals of joy radiated around the car.

Christina and Jacob promised to come by later that evening for dinner, as soon as they made sure Scarlett was handling things okay. Landon was surprised when Parker didn't put up much of a fight. Even the kind gesture he had to dig deep to offer wasn't well received, but maybe the guy needed time to process. Landon knew they hadn't seen the last of Parker, but for now, the court was on his side. The judge had taken Parker's dismissal as a nonstarter and awarded custody to Landon.

Before he made the turn onto the road to their cabin, Landon was forced to pull to the side of the road to let an ambulance and a police cruiser pass. They were moving quickly, and before he got back on the road he shot a text to Christina.

Instead of texting him back, she called. "Hey, Landon. Dispatch just got a call about a car accident at the edge of town. It sounds like Parker's rental based on the description. They're saying a male was driving, female in the passenger seat. We're headed there now."

Landon peered into the backseat. He promised and swore to protect her. Instead of racing to the scene with the baby, he took her home to the cabin. When word came later that night that Parker and Sasha had succumbed to their injuries, Landon allowed himself to breathe. It wasn't the end he was hoping for, but the idea of such anger being in Ember's life, didn't sit well either. As he put Ember in her crib, Landon thought back to where everything started. Life changes in the blink of an eye, and sometimes, reflects its positivity in a heartbeat.

Acknowledgments

Shattered Yesterdays is my book baby and I have spent the better part of the last five years nurturing it many times over. I've sent it out into the world only for it to return and have to continue nurturing it until it was ready. The patience of my readers (that's you) is something I'll never be able to thank you all enough for.

To my sweet friends and extended family, I cherish you and your support so much. Thank you for being in my life, even on those difficult days.

Especially Andrew, Keira, and Tobias; my tribe, my ride or dies. Thank you for having my back on those late nights where I missed cuddles or didn't come to bed until two a.m. I promise more cuddle time to come. Your support while I figure out this new path means more to me than you'll ever know.

Finally, to my readers, thank you for reading this story. If you've read all the editions; my heart is so full of love for you.

For news & updates on my writing, come hang out with me over on my FB page. Grab your favorite beverage and come join me at the Nano Springs Bookshop & Cafe: a virtual gathering place for people in all walks of life who enjoy books and community comfort.

https://www.facebook.com/nanospringsbc

About the Author

Sarah Louise Dale was born and raised along the Gulf Coast in a small town in Florida. As a child, Sarah's nose was always in a book and preferred other people's stories than the one she was living. A book always took her to a new world, begging to be explored.

When she's not drafting new novels, Sarah can be found advocating for homeschoolers, enjoying her family, and embracing God's purpose for her.

In her spare time, Sarah enjoys reading Women's Fiction and Historical Romance, taking photographs of the world around her, and meeting new people.

Sarah Louise Dale loves to hear from her readers. You can email her at thesweetteamama@yahoo.com.

Visit her website at www.thesweetteamama.com and be sure to check out Sarah's FB page for more news, updates, and book recommendations.

Your feedback is like a special gift to an author. Thank you for reading, *Shattered Yesterdays*.

f facebook.com/nanospringsbc

a amazon.com/Shattered-Yesterdays-Sarah-Louise-Dale/dp/1732011451

Made in United States
North Haven, CT
23 July 2023

39384477R00104